Deepwater Oil
Drillin on the Moon

By
Tom McAuliffe

NEXT STOP PARADISE
PUBLISHING
Fort Walton Beach, Florida, USA

Deepwater Oil
Drillin on the Moon

by Tom McAuliffe

First EDITION - 2024

For more information email:
bookinfo@nextstopparadise.com

WWW.AUTHORTOMMCAULIFFE.COM

<u>Dedications</u>

For everyone who works
on the Rigs in the Gulf.

And to the Families of the
Deepwater Horizon

**100% of the Profits of this book will be
donated to The Gulf of Mexico Alliance**

https://gulfofmexicoalliance.org

TABLE OF CONTENTS

COREXIT, Follow the Moola, Deep
Drilling, Working on the Moon

PREFACE

It's been almost 15 years since the world's largest oil spill in the Gulf of Mexico and it could happen again. The devastating consequences of our dependence on fossil fuels in hindsight is now even clearer. This is even more true when one considers that they're still drilling in deep water a mile down which is equivalent to drilling on the moon!

The explosion took the lives of 11 rig workers with the well unleashing roughly 3.19 million barrels of crude oil into the Gulf (2.4 million gallons per day!) and flowing for 87 days. The spill fouled more than 1,200 miles of shoreline across Louisiana, Mississippi, Alabama, and Texas. The site of the oil slick totaled more than 43,000 square miles (equal to the size of Virginia). Federal fisheries were closed in the Gulf of Mexico erasing the livelihoods Fishermen losing hundreds of millions of dollars in commercial fishing revenue.

The impacts of the disaster continue to reverberate throughout the Gulf and South even today, 15 years later. While I understand we must meet America's energy needs this was a perfect example of the fossil fuel industry's reckless pursuit of profit. We are allowing them to pollute our waters while making billions. The oil companies also continue to drill in public waters. My problem is that they expect the taxpayers to foot the bill for cleaning up their messes. A recent report by the U.S.

Government Accountability Office (GAO) indicated more than 2,700 wells and 500 platforms are actively deteriorating and are in need of being scrapped. And the Disaster was not an isolated incident since 2010 millions more gallons of oil have spilled into the Gulf.

The anniversary of the disaster can be an opportunity to re-examine our addiction to oil. With peak production being reached back in the 1980s, isn't it time to fully incentivize alternatives and phase out our reliance on polluting industries? America is 4% of the world's population but uses more than 20% of the oil. One can only hope that we will take this opportunity to reflect upon what happened, where we are and where we need to go.

Early in 2010 we moved from Hawaii back to the state of Florida and my wife and I purchased our dream home right on the water. With the luck of the Irish, a few months later in the Spring of 2010 the world's largest oil spill occurred about 150 miles away and right down the gulf coast from our new home. Caused by a catastrophic blowout accident on an offshore deep drilling rig it sent shockwaves rippling through the Gulf coast, leaving environmental and economic devastation in its wake. (Note: For the sake of our story we'll call the rig the 'Deepwater Sky' to avoid any legal entanglements and we will refer to that company from England as simply 'the Oil Company' or 'the

Corporation' and the rig ownership for the sake of our semi-fictional tale will be 'TransSea Corp.').

This event caused serious problems for my family and I. While this is not a 100% factual account we include documented details as well as our fictional story of what might have been said or done. I hope you enjoy it and it moves you to help protect the ocean and the world we live in. Scientists continue to study the long-term impacts. The memory of that fateful night serves as a sobering reminder of the risks inherent in our relentless pursuit of oil beneath the sea to meet America's energy needs.

America has treated the Gulf of Mexico as its sewer for hundreds of years even before this. Now it's 15 years after the spill and the Gulf is just not the same. And that's not me saying it, but Scientists and most importantly, folks who have lived on and fished these waters for generations. Reports in early 2012 indicated that the well was still leaking. Since the spill not one piece of legislation related to Oil drilling safety has passed Congress. Not one. There are more than 4500 platforms operating in the Gulf as I write this and we continue to act as if Oil is an unlimited resource. My question is…
Will we ever learn?

See you on or in the water!

FORWARD

On April 20, 2010, the Deepwater Horizon the world's largest oil rig exploded off the Gulf Coast, killing 11 people and injuring 17. This began an 87-day spill that spewed 3.19 million barrels, or nearly 134 million gallons, into the Gulf of Mexico. It fouled the coast from Florida to Texas launching a decade long environmental and legal battle.

The event started at 9:45 p.m. 41 miles off the Louisiana coast. At the time of the explosion the rig was drilling but was not 'in production'. It was an exploring rig and not a pumping rig. The job of the 126 men onboard was to find the oil and then move on so another rig could come in, set up and begin to pump the oil out.

After burning for more than a day, the platform sank on April 22, 2010 into more than 5000' of water. The precise cause of the explosion and fire that led to the oil spill is still under investigation even all these years later. Interviews with rig workers that were there suggest that a bubble of methane gas escaped from the well, shot up the drill column, expanding quickly as it burst through several seals and barriers before exploding. A series of stunning failures, including the heralded Blowout Preventer, and overall unpreparedness added up to what was to become the largest environmental disaster in the history of man with 11 dead, dozens injured, billions of dollar lost and with the release of more than 200,000+ barrels of crude oil into the Gulf.

As the black tide crept ever closer to our homes, residents of the Gulf Coast knew that they had to act fast to protect themselves and their fellow sea creatures from the impending disaster. With courage and determination, they rallied their friends organizing a desperate rescue mission to evacuate as many birds, turtles and marine life as possible to safety. As the oil slick spread like a dark stain across the ocean's surface, most refused to give up hope. With each passing day, they pushed themselves to the brink of exhaustion, scouring the coastline searching for stranded animals along with blobs of oil and tar balls to clean up. It was a mess. And the remedies were slow in coming if at all.

The Platform, built in Korea, was drilling an exploratory well in the Macondo Prospect more than a mile down and about 41 miles off the coast of Louisiana. The drilling operation, a routine feat for those onboard, was reaching its final stages. But deep within the Earth, at around 18,360 feet below sea level, about 3 miles down, a reservoir of crude oil and natural gas was building up pressure silently, relentlessly and catastrophically. It was all equivalent to drilling for oil… on the moon!

The methane gas from the well breach ignited and within 36 hours, the rig succumbed to the inferno and sank, leaving behind an environmental catastrophe of unprecedented scale. The well was now uncontrollably spewing oil into the Gulf and did so unabated for almost three months.

The slick spread rapidly, creating a toxic blanket that choked marine life, fouled shorelines, and disrupted ecosystems from the deep sea Gulf to the coastal marshes. Some say that while the Oil was bad it was the Oil Dispersant used for clean up that was even more harmful both to the sea life and to people involved in the 'clean up'. The impacts were immediate and devastating both environmentally and economically as local businesses shut down. Dolphins and sea turtles struggled to breathe, their bodies coated in the thick, suffocating oil. Brown pelicans, recently removed from the endangered species list, found their feathers matted and useless, leaving them unable to fly or hunt. Entire fisheries were closed, cutting off the livelihoods of thousands of Gulf residents.

Efforts to contain and clean up the spill were monumental, involving tens of thousands of workers, hundreds of vessels, and a flotilla of planes dropping dispersants over the slick. The media captured images of beaches smothered in tar, marshes blackened by oil, and birds struggling in the contaminated waters. It was a stark reminder of the fragile balance between our insatiable need for oil and gas and nature's protection.

The legal and financial aftermath was equally massive. That Oil company (I'm still so pissed I won't even say their name and would never buy gas there) faced billions in fines and claims, with the spill's total cost estimated to exceed $100 billion—a small fraction of what they earn every year. The disaster prompted widespread condemnation and supposedly led to significant changes in regulations governing offshore drilling and a renewed focus on safety and environmental protection in the oil and natural gas industries.

The night was unusually still in the Gulf of Mexico in the Spring of 2010. Stars blinked faintly above the sprawling expanse of the sea, and the 'Deep H20 Horizon' drilling rig floated like an iron titan, its massive frame a testament to human ingenuity, ambition, and hubris. Beneath the water's surface, more than a mile down on the sea floor, the Gulf holds a different story—one of geological pressure and untamed forces ready to break free.

CHAPTER 1

The Black Stuff
A
Brief History of Oil Rigs

The story of oil extraction in the United States began on land, with the first commercial oil well drilled in 1859 in Titusville, Pennsylvania. This event marked the dawn of the oil age, setting the stage for a global industry that would fuel the world's economies, power its industries, and reshape its geopolitics. However, as oil demand grew, so did the need to explore new frontiers to find it. By the early 20th century, oil companies had begun to exhaust easily accessible onshore reserves, leading them to consider the vast, untapped resources beneath the ocean.

The concept of drilling for oil offshore was, at first, met with skepticism. The ocean was unpredictable, and the technology of the time was inadequate for such an endeavor. Yet, the lure of potential oil wealth pushed engineers and entrepreneurs to experiment with new methods to reach the black gold beneath the seabed. These early pioneers of offshore drilling faced a host of challenges, from harsh weather conditions to the complexities of drilling in a marine environment. But their persistence and ingenuity would eventually lead to the development of the first offshore oil rigs, setting the stage for a revolution in energy production.

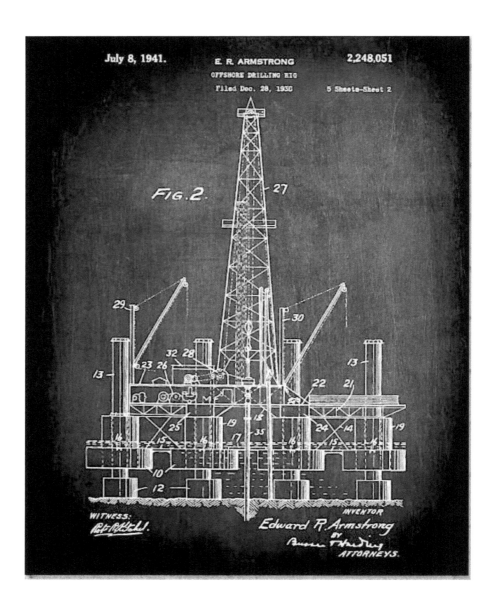

July 8, 1941.   E. R. ARMSTRONG   2,248,051
                    OFFSHORE DRILLING RIG
                     Filed Dec. 28, 1938   5 Sheets-Sheet 2

FIG.2.

WITNESS:

INVENTOR
Edward R. Armstrong
BY
ATTORNEYS.

The first attempts to drill for oil offshore were relatively modest. In the 1890s, in the Summerland oil field off the coast of California, wooden piers extended from the shore into the ocean, supporting derricks that drilled into the seabed beneath shallow waters. These early efforts were limited by the technology of the time, which allowed drilling only in very shallow waters close to the shore. Nevertheless, these wooden platforms represented a significant step forward in drilling for oil.

It wasn't until the 1930s that more sophisticated offshore drilling operations began to emerge. In 1937, a company called Pure Oil, in partnership with Superior Oil Company, constructed the first freestanding offshore oil platform in the Gulf of Mexico, off the coast of Louisiana. This platform was built in 14 feet of water, a remarkable feat at the time. The rig was a simple wooden structure, essentially an extension of the methods used in the Summerland field, but it marked the beginning of serious offshore exploration in the Gulf of Mexico.

This early platform was vulnerable to the elements, and its construction highlighted the challenges of working offshore. Harsh weather conditions, waves, and corrosion were constant threats, and the logistical difficulties of transporting materials and workers to and from the platform added to the complexity. Despite these challenges, the platform was a success, proving that offshore drilling was not only possible but also potentially lucrative.

The outbreak of World War II brought a temporary halt to the expansion of offshore drilling. In the years immediately following the war, the oil industry resumed its offshore ambitions with renewed vigor. The technological advancements of the war years, combined with the increasing demand for oil in the post-war economy, drove the development of more sophisticated offshore drilling platforms. These new platforms were built with steel instead of wood, and they were capable of withstanding the harsh conditions of the open ocean.

The late 1940s marked a significant turning point in the history of offshore drilling. In 1947, Kerr-McGee Oil Industries, in partnership with Phillips Petroleum and Stanolind Oil & Gas, made history by constructing the first true offshore oil platform that was completely out of sight of land. This platform, known as the Kermac 16, was located in the Gulf of Mexico, 10.5 miles off the coast of Louisiana in 18 feet of open water, a pioneering achievement. It demonstrated that oil could be extracted from beneath the ocean in deeper waters, far from shore, and it opened up vast new areas for exploration. The Gulf of Mexico, in particular, became a focal point for offshore drilling, as oil companies rushed to stake their claims in the promising new frontier.

During the 1950s and 1960s, the oil industry made significant advances in offshore drilling technology, driven by the increasing demand for oil and the need to access deeper and more remote reserves. The 1950s saw the introduction of mobile offshore drilling units (MODUs), which could be moved from one location to another. One of the first MODUs was the "Mr. Charlie," a submersible rig built by the Ocean Drilling and Exploration

Company (ODECO) in 1954. 'Mr. Charlie' could be floated to a drilling site and then submerged to rest on the seabed, providing a stable platform for drilling operations. This innovation significantly increased the flexibility and efficiency of offshore drilling operations, as rigs could be relocated as needed to explore new areas.

During the 1960s, the oil industry continued to push the boundaries of offshore drilling, exploring deeper waters and more remote locations. The Gulf of Mexico remained a hub of activity, with numerous new platforms being constructed and large oil fields being discovered. The success of offshore drilling in the Gulf spurred interest in other regions, leading to exploration in areas like the North Sea, California, and the shallow waters of the Middle East.

The challenges of deepwater drilling are pronounced. As offshore drilling technology advanced, oil companies began to explore the possibility of drilling in even deeper waters, beyond the continental shelf. Deepwater drilling presented a new set of challenges, as platforms had to be designed to operate in depths of thousands of feet, far beyond the reach of traditional rig structures.

One of the first solutions to the challenges of deepwater drilling was the development of the semi-submersible rig. These rigs, which were first introduced in the 1960s, are designed to float on the surface of the water while being anchored to the seabed using long, heavy chains or cables. The semi-submersible design allows the rig to remain stable even in rough seas, making it ideal for deepwater operations around the world.

Another significant innovation in deepwater drilling was the development of dynamic positioning systems. These systems use computer-controlled thrusters to keep a drilling rig or vessel in position over a well bore, even in deep water where traditional anchoring methods are not feasible. Dynamic positioning technology was a critical advancement that enabled the oil industry to drill in increasingly deep and remote locations.

By the 1970s and 1980s, deepwater drilling had become a major focus of the offshore oil industry. The Gulf of Mexico remained at the forefront of this trend, with oil companies investing heavily in the development of new deepwater platforms and technologies. During this period, the industry began to discover and develop some of the largest and most productive oil fields in the Gulf, most of which were located in deepwater areas far from shore.

As oil exploration moved into ever deeper waters, traditional fixed platforms became impractical. In response, the oil industry developed a new generation of floating platforms, capable of operating in depths of thousands of feet.

One of the most important types of floating platforms is the tension leg platform (TLP), which was first introduced in the 1980s. TLPs are anchored to the seabed using long, vertical tethers, which provide stability by keeping the platform in tension. This design allows TLPs to remain stable in deep water while still being able to move with the waves, reducing stress on the structure.

Another key innovation in floating platform design was the spar platform, first deployed in the Gulf of Mexico in the 1990s. Spar platforms are tall, cylindrical structures that float vertically in the water, with most of their mass submerged below the surface. This design provides excellent stability and allows spar platforms to operate in very deep water.

The development of floating platforms revolutionized drilling, enabling the oil industry to meet America's growing energy needs by accessing previously unreachable oil reserves in deep waters around the world. Today offshore drilling in the Gulf produces about 15% of the crude oil and 2.3% of the natural gas production in the USA.

CHAPTER 2

The Deepwater Sky
Largest Rig in the World!

The helicopter's rotors whipped through the air with a deafening hum, its vibrations coursing through my bones as we crossed the open sea. TJ Johnson stared out the window, watching the ocean below ripple under the cloud-choked sky. It stretched out in all directions, an endless expanse of steel-blue water. Somewhere in the distance, the horizon blurred into a thin line where the water met the sky. That's where the oil platform was waiting.

TJ Johnson gripped the seat's armrests tighter, knuckles white under the weight of anxiety and

<u>For You Are with Me</u>
(A prayer for those in the oil industry)

**Fill me up Lord. In this oilfield,
amidst the toil, barrenness and
isolation, for thou are
with me always.**

anticipation. The pilot had said it would take thirty minutes from shore, but time felt elastic, stretching out as the platform drew nearer. TJ Johnson caught his first glimpse of it—a massive steel behemoth rising out of the ocean like something from a science fiction novel. A maze of scaffolding, cranes, and piping towering above the waves. Johnson was close enough to make out the workers, tiny specks moving around the deck, their hard hats flashing bright yellow even from this distance.

"First time?" The man seated next to him gave a knowing grin. His face was tanned and worn, marked with the lines of someone who had spent years out here in the Gulf of Mexico. He had the kind of calm that only came from experience, a stark contrast to the knot of nerves twisting in the new comers stomach sitting across the aisle.

"Yep," Johnson nodded, forcing a smile as he asked above the sound of the chopper. "Any advice?"

"Stay alert. The platform's like a living thing—it'll test you. Watch your step, watch your head, and watch each other's backs." Rig Boss Jason Marshall paused, glancing back out the window. "It can be overwhelming at first. But you'll get used to it."

TJ Johnson wasn't so sure. From the safety of the helicopter, the platform looked like a city in the middle of nowhere, bustling with machinery and chaos. His thoughts spiraled into questions that Johnson hadn't stopped to think about during training. What if he couldn't keep up? What if he made a mistake? The instructors had warned about the dangers—one wrong move, one missed detail, and things could go south quickly.

The helicopter banked sharply to the right, descending now. The huge platform, the world's largest, loomed larger and larger until it swallowed the sky. The chopper thudded down onto the landing pad, the rotors slowing but still roaring overhead. The door slid open, and the hot salty ocean air rushed in, carrying with it the smell of oil, grease, and metal. TJ Johnson stepped out, his boots clanging against the steel deck. The platform swayed gently beneath my feet, rocking with the rhythm of the sea. It felt alien, this solid thing that wasn't supposed to move.

"Welcome to the rig," a voice boomed over the roar of the chopper. A burly man in a bright orange coverall extended his hand. "TJ Johnson? I'm Juan Martinez, Drill Shack Supervisor. You must be the new hire guy, right?"

"That's me," TJ said, shaking his hand.

Martinez gave him a once-over, eyes narrowing like he was sizing him up. "Ever worked offshore before?" he asked.

"Nope. First time," TJ Johnson admitted.

Martinez let out a short chuckle. "Figured. You got that look. Don't worry, you'll get the hang of it. Just keep your wits about you and try not to get killed. Ain't nobody but us out here on the Moon!" He motioned for Johnson to follow as he led him across the deck, his heavy boots thudding with the certainty of someone who knew every inch of this hot and loud place.

As they moved along, the enormity of the platform began to hit Johnson again. Pipes snaked overhead and along the ground, carrying who-knew-what to different sections of the rig. Massive cranes groaned under the weight of cargo, swinging supplies over the deck. The crew moved like clockwork, everyone with a job to do, everyone in sync with each other. Johnson felt out of place in his clean, unblemished clothes. He was a rookie and green in every sense.

Martinez stopped near a hatch. "You'll be working down in the engine room for your first few weeks. It's hot, loud, and about as unforgiving as it gets. If you can hack it there you'll have a future here. We'll start with the basics. Sound good?"

"Yeah, sounds good." Johnson's voice didn't betray the unease bubbling beneath the surface, but it was there, lingering in his every thought. Had he bitten off more than he could handle?

He pushed open the door, and the sound of machinery slammed into him like a wall. The heat followed—thick, oppressive, carrying the scent of oil and something else, something chemical. Inside, it was a different world. Gauges, dials, and control panels lined the walls, with workers moving from station to station, adjusting, tweaking, ensuring everything was running like it should. It felt claustrophobic compared to the open deck.

"You'll shadow Harris today," Martinez shouted over the noise, nodding toward a tall man in grease-streaked overalls. "He'll show you the ropes. Pay attention!"

Harris turned, wiping his hands on a rag. He gave the newcomer a once-over, much like Martinez had, but there was no grin this time, just a grunt of acknowledgment. "Hope you're ready to sweat, kid! Just think of it as your own personal sauna," he said.

Johnson nodded, though in his gut he wasn't sure he was fully ready for any of this. The days ahead would test him—physically and mentally. Out here, in the middle of the Gulf, there was no room for error. The platform was a machine, always hungry, always demanding. And now, TJ Johnson was gonna try to be a part of it. He was to start as a 'Roustabout' which is basically a Go-Fer and after 2-3 years he'd move up to 'Roughneck' and with more experience he could move to being 'Pumpman' and after about 5 years be might be a 'Driller' at about $75k a year.

Months passed and the only thing that disrupted the endless expanse of cobalt sky and the Gulf water at the end of the horizon was the looming silhouette of the massive Deepwater Sky oil rig. A floating city of steel and machinery, the rig stood like a sentinel in the Gulf of Mexico. It was a demonstration of the human capacity for ambition, inventiveness and hubris. The sun, low in the sky, cast long shadows across the decks. These shadows painted everything in bright shades of gold and amber. Before the storm, there was always period of calm.

While Rig Boss Marshall watched the sun sink lower into the water, he leaned against the railing and dangled a cigarette from his lips. The evening was peaceful, and the air was thick with the aroma of oil and salt. The rhythmic hum of the machinery had been the background of his life for more than twenty years, and it was a melody that he had grown accustomed to hearing. He released a cloud of smoke, allowing the wind to catch it and propel it upwards into the heavens.

"What's up, Marshall ? Who's coming?"

The sound of Tommy "TJ" Johnson's voice pierced through the silence. As he stood by the entrance to the mess hall, the young driller wore a smile that was reminiscent of a child on his first day of school.

He pushed back his hard hat, revealing a tangle of unruly blonde hair all over his head. He was hard not to like and most of the drill team did.

As Marshall responded, he did not turn around and said, "In a minute." It was true that he liked TJ, and in fact, he liked the majority of the guys on the rig, but tonight he needed some time to himself. The day's length left a lingering sense of unease, the kind of thing that gnawed at the back of his mind. His gut instinct told him that something was wrong, but he was unable to ID it and shake the feeling.

For a brief moment, TJ lingered, his smile beginning to waver. "Big meeting tonight Boss?"

As Marshall finally managed to stub out his cigarette on the metal railing, he gave nod. "Yep the oil company big cheese Mercer is flyin in to ream my ass because we're so far behind," he explained.

"I'd hate to be you!" responded a grinning Johnson.

Daniel Mercer. Simply hearing the name was enough to put Marshall in a state of gloom. Mercer was an oil executive with a Harvard degree, seemingly successful on paper, yet his ability to make decisions from a desk, oblivious to the reality of being in the middle of the Gulf, surrounded by nothing but water and pressure, was unmatched. Mercer was arriving having flown in directly from the corporate headquarters in Europe, to check on the rig's progress. Those who had never set foot on a rig in their lives had set an arbitrary deadline. Mercer was here to push for faster drilling at least this was the rumor that circulated among the crew.

It seemed as though young TJ Johnson was reading Marshall's mind when he said, "Isn't Mercer just doin his job?" the young rookie asked earnestly.

The response from Marshall was a grunt. Yes, Mercer was just going about his job but his haste just might get a bunch of guys killed. Johnson pushed himself off the railing and began walking in the direction of the mess hall. Inside the chow hall, the crew gathered around long tables, their plates piled high with whatever the cooks had managed to scrape together. The room was buzzing with an atmosphere of conversation. The aroma of fried chicken and potatoes filled the air, yet Marshall's appetite remained unsatisfied.

Having arrived 20 minutes ago Daniel Mercer was standing at the other end of the room, holding a clipboard in his hand and having a conversation with a couple of the senior TransSea engineers. Despite the dust and grime present on the rig, his dark hair, pulled back into a tight bun, was immaculate, as was his out of place suit. Mercer was rather tall. His appearance was so out of place, it was akin to a bunch of fine china in a room filled with bulls.

"Marshall!" Mercer yelled out as soon as Mercer caught sight of him, his voice piercing through the din of the various conversations. "Can we have a a few moments to talk?"

Marshall gave a slight nod. After muttering under his breath, "Here it comes…" he made his way over to Mercer and the two of them found a semi-quiet corner to talk things over.

Mercer immediately asked, "How's everything looking?" ignoring any small talk. Mercer scanned Marshall's face with his sharp and calculated eyes, looking for any signs of hesitation.
"Everything is very fine," Marshall said in a level tone. "There have been some pressure fluctuations, but nothing we can't handle. We know things are a little behind schedule."

A frown appeared on his face as Mercer scrawled something on his clipboard. "Ahhhh it's way more than a little sir… almost 60 days! What fluctuations?" he asked.

There was a tightening of Marshall's jaw. "There's nothing out of the ordinary for a rig of this size at this depth. One thing at a time. We're running tests."

Mercer narrowed his eyes and pressed his lips together. "But it's not normal?"

Marshall crossed his arms and said,"It's not out of the ordinary especially at this depth. At more than a mile down it's like drilling on the damn Moon! Look, we've been drilling deeper than ever before so please keep in mind that there will be some variations," he said.

There was now hesitation in Mercer's eyes. "Marshall, handling it is different from *controlling* it, yes? We've a very restrictive timetable as you know. To be successful, we must achieve our goals before the end of the quarter. What we need to know now… is your team capable of delivering?"
Marshall replied, "That's the plan!" but the words began to feel heavy in his mouth even as he spoke them. "But it's imperative that we also keep safety in mind. There's no point in meeting deadlines if someone gets hurt… right?"

The expression on his face was indecipherable as Mercer glanced down at his clipboard and then back at him. "Naturally, safety is of the utmost importance. However, we must also keep in mind that our objective is irreversible. The company is spending millions of dollars on this project every day and we expect to see results," he said emphatically. "Kick some ass and get it done!"

Marshall didn't respond as there was really nothing else to say. He was proficient at the game of corporate politics and bullshit. It was not his intention to make new friends or to teach the complexities of deep-sea drilling, not while Mercer was here anyway. He knew full well that Mercer's purpose in being out on the rig was basically to be in his face. The Corporation wanted to ensure that the drilling finished up ASAP so that the rig could move on to the next exploratory well. Time is money.

"Just make sure that your team is on point and let's finish this damn thing up," Mercer said, his tone becoming slightly more animated. "We at corporate simply can't afford to have any more delays."

With a neutral expression on his face, Marshall gave a slight nod. "We're gonna get it done," he said. Even as he said it he knew that it was a long road from here to pulling the rig and moving to the next site. His more than 20 years out here said to him that it was not going to be so easy and that something, and he could not put his finger on it, just didn't feel right with the rig.

After giving Mr Mercer a curt nod and continuing to observe him briefly, Mercer simply and dismissively turned and walked away, his heels clicking against the metal floor surface. The knot in Marshall's stomach tightened as he watched him leave. Turning his attention back to the room, he saw that the crew was laughing and chatting, completely oblivious to the tension that was building up between TransSea and the oil company. Despite the fact that he ought to have felt relieved, the uneasiness only grew.

There was a problem, and he couldn't shake the feeling that they were all perched on the brink of a cliff. He was convinced that something was wrong on the Deepwater Sky platform. But what? All he knew for sure was that to fall, you only need one wrong step when standing this close to the edge. He cast a final glance through the small porthole out to where the sun was starting to set. The next day, they would drill even deeper into sea bed, more than a mile down, to find more oil. But tonight things on the Deepwater Sky were peaceful; the evening was clear, the stars were bright, the Gulf was calm and the rig stood tall against night… for now.

CHAPTER 3

Caution, Pressure and Mud... Oh My!
Go Fever is Catching

When morning arrived, there was a thick fog that clung to the rig, making it difficult to see the horizon and drowning out the sounds of the Gulf of Mexico. As Jason Marshall walked the entire length of the deck, the sound of his boots causing a thud against the metal grating reverberated throughout the otherwise silent space. During these early hours, when the rig was still quiet and the crew was still attempting to shake off the last remnants of sleep, he preferred to be with them. It provided him with the opportunity to reflect and get a sense of the day before the deafening din and disorder took over.

He made his way to one of the control panels and checked the device's pressure readings, as was his custom. Despite the fact that the numbers on the screen gave off a steady green glow and were within the high end of the normal range, he did not feel reassured. It seemed as if the morning's tranquility was exerting an excessive amount of effort to persuade him that everything was in order.

Because Marshall had been on a sufficient number of rigs, he was aware that when everything appeared to be in perfect order, it was typically just the universe getting ready to deliver a surprise sucker punch. "Most roughnecks just wanna do three things anyway; Fight, Fuc and Trip Pipe! ('Tripping Pipe'

Methane Gas from the well hole

was rig slang for drilling.)" he said to himself. Working on this rig now had him talking to himself!

Suddenly, TJ's voice broke the silence and said, "Morning, boss." Even though his eyes were bleary from sleep, the young driller approached with the same level of energy that he always had. "It's quiet out here, isn't it?" he said.

While Marshall was looking out over the Gulf horizon, he muttered, "Too quiet. Is there anything going on at your end?"

TJ, who had become a reliable member of the drill team, rubbed the back of his neck and shrugged his shoulders. "Not much of a concern I guess. The only issue is the vibration in the drill pipe. At this point, that has been ongoing for a few days. Despite the fact that the guys claim it's not a big deal, it's extremely annoying."

Marshall now wore a frown. "Have you reported this? Why wasn't I told?! This is dangerous you know? We are going way too fast!"

TJ's response was, "Yeah, I told Martinez," referring to the person in charge of drill shack. "According to him, the drill bit is likely too worn. We should replace it later today. That'll fix 'er!"

Although Marshall gave a slight nod, the response did not sit well with him. "TJ, please help me closely monitor that situation. I need to know as soon as possible if it continues to get worse. OK?"

"Good enough." TJ gave him a thumbs up and then proceeded toward the drill floor, his steps becoming lighter now that he had handed off the responsibilities for the problem's the Drill Team was experiencing and could enjoy the rest of his shift.

Marshall stayed at the control panel, monitoring the numbers and listening to the low hum of the rig as it came to life. Although TJ's description of the vibration was not unusual, it required immediate attention instead of delaying it. He made a mental note to check in with Martinez and inquire about the possibility of accelerating the process of replacing the drill bit. Changing one usually took a few hours.

As members of the crew arrived for the Day shift, the rig transformed from a silhouette in the fog into a bustling hive of activity. The atmosphere was filled with the sounds of machinery, the clanking of tools, and voices yelling orders and responses. There was an underlying sense of unease that continued to linger, and it began to gnaw at Marshall's stomach. But this always happened at the end of an evolution, it went with the territory and the responsibilities.

The clanging of wrenches and the roar of machinery filled the air as TJ tightened a bolt on the pipe flange. His hands were slick with grease, the heat of the engine room pressing down on him like a physical weight. Out the monitoring window and across the platform, he saw Marshall inspecting one of the massive pressure valves. They hadn't exchanged more than a few words since TJ started months ago—Marshall wasn't much of a talker. But now, there was a tension between them, something unspoken hanging heavy in the air and Johnson didn't know why.

Suddenly, Marshall slammed his wrench down onto the grated floor with a sharp clatter, his face red under his hard hat. TJ Johnson looked up, startled.

"You gonna tighten that thing or just stare at it all day?" Marshall growled, his voice cutting through the noise like a blade.

Johnson felt his pulse quicken. "I'm doing it right, Mr. Marshall. Relax."

"Right?" Marshall scoffed, wiping the sweat from his brow. "There's a right way and then there's a fast way, and you're doing neither. You keep dragging your feet, we're gonna be at this all day and we will never finish this damn drill."

"I'm following the procedures!" Johnson shot back, standing up from his crouch. He could feel his frustration building. "You told me to take my time and do it right. Now you want me to rush?"

Marshall stepped closer, his eyes narrowing. "This ain't about taking time, kid. It's about doing your damn job without second-guessing everything. We're on a tight schedule and our asses are on the line now."

Johnson could feel it rising in his chest, a mix of anger and anxiety. "You're the one always harping on safety! Now you want me to ignore that just to meet some arbitrary deadline? This platform's dangerous enough without cutting corners!"

Marshall shook his head, his lips curling into a sneer. "You think you know everything after six months, huh? You young guys just don't get it. You think safety's just about following rules and slowing down every time something doesn't look perfect. But this platform's not a classroom son. Out here, we have to balance speed *and* safety. If we stop every time someone's got a gut feeling, we'll never get anything done!" he said.

Johnson felt his fists clenching, his voice rising with his frustration. "That's bullshit, Marshall! You told me on my very first day that one mistake could kill someone. You said we 'watch each other's backs'. But now you're acting like none of that matters because we're 'on a schedule'? Lemme be real clear for you, kay? I ain't risking my life or anyone else's just because you and corporate are now in a rush."

Marshall's eyes flashed, his voice dropping to a dangerous low. "You think I don't know that? I've been on this rig for ten years. I've seen guys get hurt —bad. I know what's at stake better than you ever will. But if you don't learn to trust your own judgment, you're gonna freeze up when it really counts. And that's when things go sideways. You don't hesitate out here."

Johnson took a step forward, matching Marshall's intensity. "It's not about hesitation. It's about not

being reckless. I'm not just another set of hands to you, am I? I'm supposed to be a part of this team, and if you don't think safety matters, then we've got a real problem. They can't have it both ways—either we do it right, or we don't do it at all."

For a moment, the two men stood there, the weight of their words hanging in the sweltering air between them. The engine room's steady hum seemed louder, the heat even more oppressive.

Marshall broke the silence first, his voice softer but no less sharp. "You really think I don't care about safety? You think I don't want you and the others to get home in one piece?" He pointed a finger at Johnson, his hand shaking. "But out here, it's not always black and white. You learn to make calls on the fly. You trust the guy next to you and hope like hell they've got the same sense. There's no time to play it safe every damn minute. Sometimes, you have to make a judgment call," he said.

Johnson met his stare, his voice steady but softening. "I get that sir I really do. But I'm not gonna make a call that costs someone their life because they're in a hurry. They might think they know better, but there's a reason those safety protocols exist. I'm not ignoring them and I know in your heart you don't want me to either."

Marshall sighed, rubbing the back of his neck. For a moment, he seemed to deflate, the fire in his eyes cooling. "Maybe I came down on ya too hard. Sorry. Things are really fucked up top side. But listen—

47

this job's about survival as much as it's about getting it done. There's always gonna be pressure from the top to meet deadlines, push harder, work faster. I guess that's how it is. But if you freeze up because you're scared of making a mistake, that's when people get hurt!"

Johnson crossed his arms, his voice still firm but less heated. "I'm not scared of making mistakes, Mr. Marshall. I'm scared of what happens when we stop caring about them!"

Marshall looked at him for a long moment, then nodded slowly. "Fair enough. Just don't get so wrapped up in the rules that you forget how to trust yourself out here. The rules don't always save you and TJ you're a good man I would hate to lose."

Johnson didn't respond right away, the tension between them finally easing. He knew Marshall was right, in his own way and that he was under a lot of pressure. Out here on the rig, everything was a balance. But he also knew he had to draw his own lines. Safety wasn't just a checklist—it was a responsibility for all.

"I'll trust myself," Johnson said finally more to himself than anyone else. "But I'm still doing all these ops by the book."

Marshall gave a short, humorless laugh, shaking his head as he picked up his wrench. "Kid, I wouldn't expect anything less,… that's the way I want it too."

Later that day around 7pm Marshall was in the platform control room, surrounded by gauges and monitors, when the first alarm went off. Though not an emergency beep, it was strong enough to get his attention. It was a low and persistent beep. He took two steps across the room and then tapped the screen once he was there. The display showed a slight rise in pressure within the well, only a few PSI higher than the anticipated range.

"Are ya seeing this, Martinez? Are you?!" Marshall asked urgently as the gauge needles rose further.

Martinez, the team's Lead Driller, was hunched over another console, remaining deeply focused on his task. Marshall called out again over his shoulder. "Damn, these readings are all over the place!"

Martinez raised his head, wiping a smear of grease from his forehead before looking up. "Yes sir, I

agree with you. These kinds of spikes have occurred on multiple occasions over the past few days. Although it's not a major issue, it is unusual. But it's not enough..." his voice trailing off.

The tone that Marshall used became more acerbic."You mean call a stoppage? (meaning to stop all drilling operations which only a few personnel on the rig can do)," he asked.

Martinez straightened his posture and moved so that he could stand next to him. "The consistency is not there. The pressure has been up and down, but it's completely unpredictable," he said. "There is no discernible pattern. We have made adjustments to the mud's weight, but it is still happening. With a frown on his face, Marshall continued to stare at the screen. "Are these damn things even working? At this point, what is the spike value and duration? Has it always been this high today?" he asked.

"It's nothing beyond the capabilities of the BOP," Martinez said, attempting to sound reassuring; however, Marshall was able to pick up on the uncertainty in Martinez's voice.

"Not the point... We've never seen anything like this before, at least not on this rig," Marshall said giving a slow nod with his thoughts racing rapidly. The BOP, also known as The Blowout Preventer, served as their final line of defense. In the event that the pressure reached an unmanageable level and they were unable to exert control over the drilling process, the BOP was supposed to seal the well and avert a catastrophe. On the other hand, Marshall and the TransSea Corp. had discovered the hard way over the years that placing an excessive amount of faith in failsafes was a risky game.

"Without further ado, let's get the team back together," Marshall advised. "My request is for a comprehensive analysis of the system.Let's check the mud, the drill string, and all other components."

"Corporate ain't gonna liiiiiike it!" Martinez said.

"Like I give a rat's ass!" responded Marshall.

Before reaching for the intercom, Martinez gave a curt nod and reached for it. Senior members of the Drill Team occupied the control room within minutes, their faces displaying a mixture of concern and curiosity. TransSea Rig Supervisor Jason Marshall briefed them in a timely manner while maintaining a measured tone at all times; however, he did not sugarcoat the situation. He said something did not feel right and that it required them to be alert, focused, and prepared to take action in the event that things went awry.

During the meeting's conclusion, Marshall was able to catch a glimpse of Daniel Mercer of the Oil company standing in the hatchway. Today was no exception to his habit of showing up when you least expected him to do so. Mercer had a way of doing it. The sound of his heels clicking softly on the deck was audible as Mercer entered the room his expression virtually unreadable and met by silence.

"Heard we're having some pressure issues." Mercer stated his arms folded across his chest.

Keeping his tone unaffected, Marshall responded, "Nothing we aren't able to deal with."

Mercer raised an eyebrow to show that he was clearly dissatisfied with this response. "Do we have reason to be concerned?" he asked.

At that moment, Marshall turned his attention back to the pressure monitor and said, "It all depends on how much faith you have in this equipment." Even though the pressure had returned to normal, the memory of that spike lingered in his mind like a splinter. "We were due for a re-fit and maintenance cycle 18 months ago as you well know," Marshall said. It was the first time the conflict between TransSea who owned the platform and the Oil Company was fully out in the open and it was done in front of the crew which was sort of a first.

In a calm and collected manner, Mercer stated, "I have a great deal of confidence in this platform and crew, Marshall." "However, I am not unaware of any real danger, certainly not enough to stop drillin'. So what's your suggestion on all this then?"

Marshall sighed and inhaled deeply and deliberated over the words he would use. "Diagnostics are currently being carried out. If the pressure levels continue to rise, we may have to shut down the well and reevaluate the situation," he asserted.mHis pupils contracted ever-so-slightly. "Because of that, we will fall behind schedule even further."

"I'm well aware," Mercer interrupted, looking directly at him. "We don't want to pressure ya!"

Marshall continued, "However, if we don't slow down, and something goes wrong, we'll be dealing with more than just a delay in product delivery."

In those brief moments, neither of them made a sound. The crew ran their checks with the low hum of computers and the soft click of keys, but Marshall could only hear his insistent heartbeat.

Mercer's expression became slightly more gentle as he examined him, revealing a hint of concern. In the end, Mercer decided to say, "Alright, Marshall. Carry out the testings required. But please keep me informed. We're way behind and HQ is not happy!"

Marshall nodded as he watched him turn and walk away, maintaining the same rigid posture Mercer had all along. He was a stiff kind of guy. Mercer was undoubtedly skilled in his work, but Marshall couldn't shake the feeling that they were on opposing sides of the same issue and goal. Mercer and the company's primary concern were the numbers, the deadlines, and the bottom line... profit. The safety of the crew and the integrity of the rig were Marshall's primary and really his only concern.

To him the oil company could wait till hell froze over rather than he endanger his team.

As the day progressed, the diagnostic results came back negative. Nothing indicated an imminent problem, and there were no significant issues. The pressure readings, on the other hand, continued to fluctuate, appearing as faint blips on the radar that refused to disappear. Marshall spent the rest of the day walking around the rig, checking in with the crew, and thoroughly inspecting the systems. After the fog lifted, a bright and glaring sun appeared, which did nothing to alleviate the tension that was building up in his chest.

By the time evening arrived, Marshall had returned to the upper decks, where the horizon was a thin line of orange against the blue that was getting deeper. The familiar burn of the cigarette did little to calm his nerves, despite the fact that he lit it and took a deep breath. While the rig was quiet again and the crew had settled into their evening routines, the feeling of unease was stronger than ever.

Mercer sent a message via walkie talkie, "Jason Marshall to the Conference Room… Marshall to the Conference Room please!"

"Roger, on my way!" came the response.

The conference room on the rig was small and bare, its walls a dull gray with flickering fluorescent lights overhead. Outside the window, the deep blue Gulf stretched to the horizon, but inside, the tension was palpable. The company oil representative, Daniel Mercer, sat across from Jason Marshall, the 15 year rig supervisor from TransSea. Between them, an ocean of unspoken resentment simmered just beneath the surface. The oil company and TransSea the rig operator hated each other fir everything from breaking production schedules to safety violations to pay and benefits for the workers. The corporation was stingy with funding and TransSea had a history of bending over and not sticking up for the workers and the rig's maintenance.

Mercer adjusted his corporate cufflinks, his suit an odd contrast to the oil-stained walls and work clothes of the rig. "Marshall," he began, his voice measured and professional, "I understand you've directed that another pressure test be done. We need to address your delays in production. Our timeline is being pushed back day after day, and it's costing both of us a whole lot of money."

Marshall leaned back in his chair, arms crossed over his chest, his oil-splattered coveralls a badge of the work Mercer never touched. He raised an eyebrow, his tone as unyielding as the steel of Marshall's rig. And the Deep[water Sky platform may have been owned by TransSea but when Marshall was onboard there was no doubt about whose rig it was.

"Is that right? Well, safety is first and we're doing everything we can. Out here, things don't move at the speed of your spreadsheets sir. We've got equipment that's barely holding together, and if you want to push us faster, you may just be askin for trouble," Marshall stated his French creole accent starting to come out.

Mercer sighed, folding his hands on the table. "Look, I understand the challenges. I really do. But this is an expensive operation. Corporate is expecting results, and they're not seeing 'em. The well's way behind schedule, and the board is already asking questions. We need more output, Marshall, it is that simple. And if you can't provide that then we will need to re-evaluate things."

110% Louisiana Creole, when Marshall got angry he would sometimes switch languages. His eyes darkened, and he straightened in his chair. His voice, usually gruff, took on a sharper edge as he switched to Creole, letting his frustration break through.

"Ou pa konprann sa kap pase isit la," he muttered. "Nou pa nan biro ou. Sa a se yon rig kap fonksyone nan kondisyon reyèl. Si ou pouse nou, nou ka kraze tout bagay."

Mercer blinked, clearly unsettled by the language switch. "Marshall, I, I don't understand…"

"I said," Marshall cutting him off and reverting briefly to English, "you keep pushing us sir and somethin's gonna break!"

Mercer's expression tightened, and he leaned forward. "We're all under pressure here, Mr.

"Mwen pap jwe ak lavi moun mwen yo pou satisfè envestisè ou yo!"

"I'm not going to gamble with my men's lives to satisfy your investors!"

TransSea Official Speaking in Louisianian Creole

Marshall. The company has invested billions into this project. Their expectation was clear—high production, on time and on budget. You're the supervisor; it's *your* responsibility to make sure that happens and you will be held accountable."

Marshall shook his head, his frustration boiling over. "Ou jis ap pale de lajan ou!" he shot back in Creole, his voice thick with anger. "Mwen ap pale de lavi moun mwen yo. Ou vle nou akselere pandan ke ekipman yo ap kraze anba nou. Men, lè bagay yo pete, se nou kap pran kou!"

"What the hell does that mean?!" Mercer responded.

"All you're talking about is money," Marshall explained. "I'm talking about the lives of *my* men. You want us to speed up while the equipment is falling apart under us. But when things blow up, we're the ones who get hurt out here while you sit your fat asses over in Houston and back in Europe!"

Mercer's tone grew icy, his eyes narrowing. "You think I don't know what's at stake? I know the risks, but TransSea is contracted to meet deadlines, and it's not delivering. And we've got investors too!"

Marshall stepped closer, his fists clenched. "Mwen pap jwe ak lavi moun mwen yo pou satisfè envestisè ou yo," he growled. "Si yon bagay mal pase sou rig la, ou pa pral isit la pou wè konsekans yo. Mwen konnen rig sa a, mwen konnen sa li ka fè!"

He switched to English. "I'm not going to gamble with my men's lives just to satisfy your goddamn investors. Period!"

Mercer adjusted his tie and straightened in his chair, clearly growing impatient. "This isn't just about you and *your* men. This is a global operation, and delays here ripple across the entire company and the whole supply chain. We need results, Marshall, and we need them fast. Do it or we'll find someone who will its that simple!"

Marshall's eyes blazed with fury, and he jabbed a finger at Mercer. "Rezilta? Sa ou rele rezilta se pwoblèm k ap monte. Mwen pa pral riske yon eksplozyon pou 'rezilta'. Ou pa ka konprann sa mwen di a paske ou pa janm pase yon jou ap travay nan chalè, nan presyon, menas ki genyen sou rig la."

"Speak English damn it!" Mercer said.

"Ok I will… as you too spoiled and stupid to know where you is!" Marshall responded with sarcasm. "If something goes wrong on this here rig, you won't be here to see it. I know this rig, I know what it and this team can handle and you don't. Results? What you call results is just trouble piling up."

Mercer's lips thinned, his tone now cold and clipped. "We'll get you the equipment fixes you need after you are done, but we need progress. Do you understand?"

Marshall took a deep breath, his fists unclenching but his gaze unwavering. "Mwen konprann," he said quietly, his Creole soft but firm. "Men, ou mèt sonje, se mwen ki konnen rig la, se mwen ki pran responsablite pou moun mwen yo. Ou ka voye kout presyon, men mwen pap voye pèsonn al mouri pou satisfè tablo kalkil ou."

"In other words?" Marshall said. "I'm not going to risk an explosion for 'results.' Period! You can't understand what I'm saying because you've never spent a day working out here in the heat and under the constant threats out here on *my* rig."

Mercer glanced out the port hole, the stormy skies, churning Gulf and 6 foot swells reflecting the storm of tension in the small conference room.

"I'll report your thoughts back to the board. We're counting on TransSea and you, Mr. Marshall," Mercer said. Without another word, he turned and walked out, leaving Marshall standing there, the weight of the conversation thick in the air. Marshall watched him go, shaking his head and muttering under his breath, "Wi, ou ka konte sou mwen... men ou pa menm konprann sa ou mande pou mwen fè."

Which meant; "You can keep up the pressure, but I'm not sending anyone to die just to satisfy your spreadsheets!" He glanced back out toward the rig, the oil-slicked steel structures jutting against the darkening sky. It all equaled a dangerous situation.

"Bagay yo ap chanje lè ou kite kote sa a," he murmured to himself. "Si ou vle viv lontan," he said with frown. "Things will change when *you* leave this place. If you want to stay alive go now!"

He walked out to the overhang outside and stood there for a considerable amount of time, watching the sun sink below the surface of the Gulf and feeling the first cool breeze of the night on his face. In contrast to the diminishing sunlight, the rig stood tall and proud in the middle of the calm sea and still air. However, Marshall knew the warning signs were all present just beneath the surface and the alarm bells were ringing quickly just like his heartbeat whenever he thought about the Deepwater Sky.

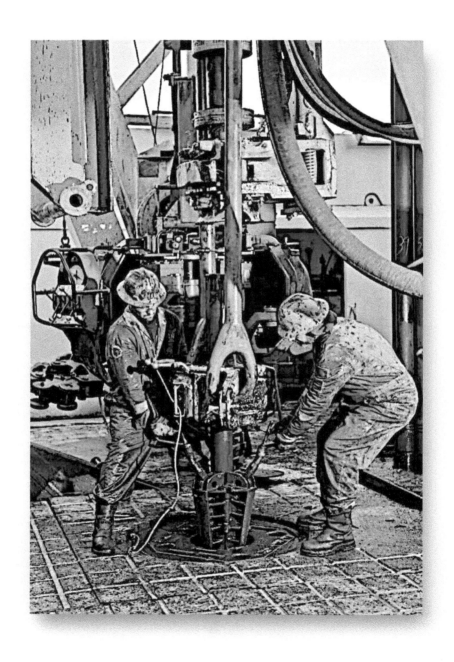

CHAPTER 4

The Blowout
Dealing with a Predictable Outcome

The night settled over the Gulf like a heavy blanket of humidity, suffocating and oppressive. It appeared as though the rig, which was typically a ray of light in the middle of the vast darkness, shrank under its weight. The tension was palpable, like a silent current that ran through the steel bones of the Deepwater Sky. The crew moved through their shifts with the mechanical precision of men who had done this a thousand times before, but the tension was now evident growing and debilitating.

When Marshall entered the drill control room, he stood there and stared at the collection of monitors that were in front of him. The glow of the screens cast strong shadows on his face, highlighting the lines of worry that had intensified over the past few days. Despite the fact that the pressure readings had returned to normal, he was unable to shake the feeling that they were just on the brink of a dangerous situation, at least for the time being.

The eyes of Martinez, who was standing next to him, were constantly moving between the screens and the paperwork that was in front of him. He murmured, "Everything is looking good," more to himself than to Marshall . "It's very encouraging."

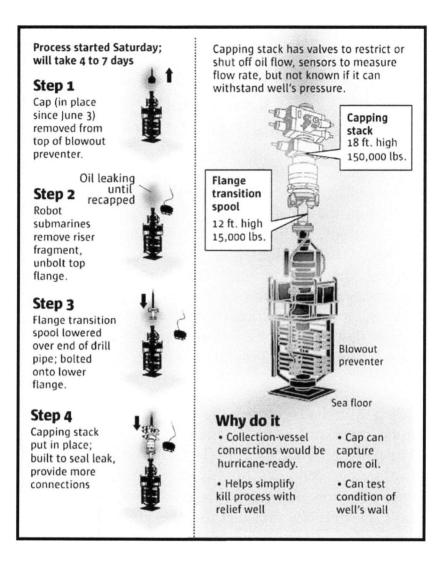

Process started Saturday; will take 4 to 7 days

Step 1

Cap (in place since June 3) removed from top of blowout preventer.

Step 2 Oil leaking until recapped

Robot submarines remove riser fragment, unbolt top flange.

Step 3

Flange transition spool lowered over end of drill pipe; bolted onto lower flange.

Step 4

Capping stack put in place; built to seal leak, provide more connections

Capping stack has valves to restrict or shut off oil flow, sensors to measure flow rate, but not known if it can withstand well's pressure.

Capping stack
18 ft. high
150,000 lbs.

Flange transition spool
12 ft. high
15,000 lbs.

Blowout preventer

Sea floor

Why do it

• Collection-vessel connections would be hurricane-ready.

• Helps simplify kill process with relief well

• Cap can capture more oil.

• Can test condition of well's wall

With a grunt, Marshall responded, his gaze remaining fixed on the monitors the entire time. He was unsure and uneasy. He finally spoke up and said, "Alright, let's ease into it," employing a tone that was low but firm. "Keep the mud weight at a constant level and pay close attention to the pressure. We don't want any surprises!" The team went about their tasks rapidly.

Martinez gave a slight nod and then communicated the instructions directly to the crew through the radio. The air was filled with the low murmur of voices and the steady hum of machinery, filling the room with buzzing activity. Marshall attempted to stifle the growing feeling of dread in his stomach by crossing his arms. It did not work.

They had replaced the drill bit earlier in the day and were now ready to resume their drilling operations in more than 5000 feet of water. The situation was supposed to be routine, just another step in a lengthy and complicated process; however, Marshall knew better than to let his guard down and let out his guard. The Gulf of Mexico was a capricious mistress who didn't tolerate arrogance or inattention.

Hours went by in a haze of information and numerical values. The machinery groaned and creaked as it thrust itself deeper into the ground, and the rig throbbed with living things' activity. Marshall fixed his gaze on the pressure gauge, watching as the needle hovered just below the potentially hazardous zone.

After that, the needle suddenly jumped without any warning.The room was filled with Marshall's barking voice. As he watched the needle continue to travel higher and higher, he felt his heart pounding in his chest. Each tick was a countdown to the impending catastrophe. The night shift was in full swing, rig workers and engineers moving to the steady rhythm of practiced and professional hands.

A Blowout Preventer

A Perfect Failure
Why the BOP Failed

On April 20, 2010, the oil rig suffered a catastrophic blowout that resulted in one of the largest environmental disasters in history. At the heart of the disaster was the failure of the Blowout Preventer (BOP)—a crucial piece of safety equipment designed to halt uncontrolled oil and gas flows. Despite its importance, the BOP on the rig failed to function as intended, leading to an unprecedented release of oil into the Gulf of Mexico. Understanding why the blowout preventer failed involves examining its design, maintenance, operational procedures, and the complex interplay of factors that contributed to its ultimate malfunction. It was not just machine error.

The Role and Design of the Blowout Preventer

A Blowout Preventer is a specialized valve assembly located on the seabed at the wellhead. Its primary function is to control and shut off the flow of oil and gas from a well in the event of a blowout—a sudden, uncontrolled release of hydrocarbons. The huge BOP is designed with multiple mechanisms, including shear rams, pipe rams, and annular preventers, each serving a specific purpose. Shear rams are meant to cut through the drill pipe and seal the well, while pipe rams seal around the drill pipe, and annular preventers seal the well bore when there is no pipe in place.

Mechanical Failures & Design Flaws

The platform's BOP was manufactured by a leading manufacturer. It was a sophisticated design, but was plagued by several mechanical issues. Reports revealed that the BOP had experienced problems with its shear rams, which are crucial for cutting and sealing the well. In the case of the Deepwater Horizon, the shear rams failed to cut through the drill pipe effectively. This failure was partly due to the drill pipe being made of high-strength steel a significant challenge for the shearing rams.

Furthermore, the BOP's control system, which relied on hydraulic fluids, was found to be deficient. The system had leaks and other malfunctions that compromised its ability to function under extreme pressure conditions. These mechanical failures were compounded by a design flaw: the BOP's shear rams were not equipped to handle the high pressures and forces involved in a deepwater blowout.

Operational & Maintenance Issues

The rigs BOP had been in operation for several years prior to the spill. Regular maintenance and testing are critical for ensuring the functionality of such equipment, but records indicated that the BOP had not undergone thorough testing or maintenance in the period leading up to the disaster. In particular, the BOP's battery-operated emergency systems, which are crucial for activating the BOP in case of a primary system failure, were found to be in poor condition.

One of the sunken platform's maneuvering thrusters now on the bottom of the Gulf.

Additionally, there were discrepancies in the operational procedures followed by the rig's crew. The crew had not conducted a proper test of the BOP's emergency systems, which could have identified potential issues before the blowout occurred. The lack of rigorous maintenance and operational checks contributed to the BOP's inability to respond effectively to the blowout.

Human Error & Decision-Making Failures

Human factors played a significant role in the BOP's failure. The decision-making process on the platform was influenced by time pressures, cost considerations, and a culture that prioritized operational efficiency over safety. In the hours leading up to the blowout, the rig crew and engineers were faced with conflicting information and high-stress conditions. They made several critical errors, including inadequate pressure tests and misinterpretation of test results.

For instance, the crew received ambiguous pressure readings that suggested a possible blowout risk, but their response was not swift or decisive enough to prevent the disaster. The failure to act on these warning signs, combined with a lack of effective communication and coordination among the crew and the onshore support team, led to a delayed and ineffective response to the impending blowout.

Regulatory and Oversight Failures

Regulatory oversight also played a role in the BOP's failure. The Minerals Management Service (MMS),

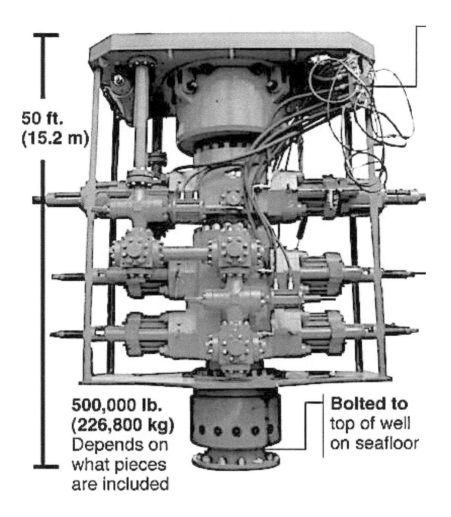

**50 ft.
(15.2 m)**

**500,000 lb.
(226,800 kg)
Depends on
what pieces
are included**

**Bolted to
top of well
on seafloor**

the regulatory body responsible for overseeing offshore drilling operations, had been criticized for its lax enforcement of safety regulations. The agency's inspection and approval processes were not sufficiently rigorous, and there were lapses in ensuring that safety equipment, such as the BOP, met the required standards.

The lack of stringent regulatory oversight meant that the BOP's design and maintenance issues were not adequately addressed. Furthermore, the culture of regulatory leniency fostered an environment where safety concerns were often overlooked or downplayed in favor of meeting operational targets and reducing costs.

Systemic Issues and Industry Practices
The failure of the BOP also reflects broader systemic issues within the offshore drilling industry. The industry's focus on cost-cutting and operational efficiency often came at the expense of safety. Companies, including the oil company, the operator of the Deepwater Horizon, faced intense pressure to maximize production and minimize expenses, which led to compromises in safety practices and equipment maintenance.

The industry's reliance on complex and expensive equipment, such as the BOP, without ensuring its reliability and effectiveness, highlights a systemic issue. The failure to invest in robust safety measures and the tendency to prioritize short-term gains over long-term safety created vulnerabilities that contributed to the disaster.

The Aftermath and Lessons Learned
In the wake of the Deepwater Horizon oil spill, extensive investigations revealed the multifaceted nature of the BOP's failure. The disaster prompted significant changes in industry practices and regulatory frameworks. New standards were

implemented to improve the design, testing, and maintenance of blowout preventers. Regulatory agencies increased oversight and enforcement to ensure that safety equipment met strict standards.

The Deepwater Horizon spill also underscored the importance of a safety culture that prioritizes risk management and proactive measures. Lessons learned from the disaster have led to improvements in emergency response procedures, equipment reliability, and regulatory oversight.

The failure of the Blowout Preventer was a tragic reminder of the consequences of inadequate safety measures, design flaws, and operational lapses. Understanding these failures provides valuable insights into the complexities of offshore drilling safety and the need for continuous improvement to prevent disasters. Which is a good thing because operations in deepwater drilling, more than a mile down. is still occurring every day in the Gulf, North Sea and elsewhere around the world.

CHAPTER 5

Into the Inferno
Too Little, Too Late

At 9:45 PM on April 20, 2010, the rhythm of the rig was shattered. A surge of mud and seawater shot up the well, a harbinger of the disaster to come. Moments later, the Blowout Preventer—a massive set of valves designed to seal the well in dire emergencies—failed. There had been problems with its hydraulics before. A little while later a large column of oil and gas erupted from the depths came up the drill pipe igniting almost instantly and engulfing most of the rig in flames.

Chaos erupted. The rig workers scrambled for their lives, their training kicking in even as fear gripped their hearts. Explosions ripped through the structure, lighting up the night sky in an inferno. The platform's alarm wailed its unheeded warning as fireballs shot into the sky, fueled by the hydrocarbons spewing from the wellhead. It took hours for rescuers to arrive, and by the time they did, the Deepwater Sky was a towering pillar of flame, its fate all but sealed.

"Shut it down!" Martinez screamed, his fingers flying across the controls. "Shut it all down now… hit the BOP! Launch the Fire Suppression Team!" The BOP did not respond to Martinez's commands.

The alarms blared, a deafening wail that sent the crew into a frenzy. Marshall grabbed the two-way radio, his voice urgent. "All hands, brace for emergency! We got a blowout comin!" But even as he said the words, he knew it was already too late.

The rig trembled violently, producing a low rumble that reverberated throughout the structure made of metal. Marshall experienced a profound and fundamental fear that caused his stomach to become knotted up. He felt it deep in his bones. He sensed the floor beneath him buckle, and the lights flickered then became super bright as power surged throughout the platform. Then, their entire world came crashing down.

An even more massive plume of oil and gas erupted

from the well, shooting fire into the sky like a geyser direct from hell itself. The air was filled with a deafening roar that filled the entire atmosphere. Both Marshall and Martinez were knocked down by the second explosion, and the control room shook like an earthquake. The pressure caused the large glass monitor window to shatter, the walls to groan, and for a brief moment, Marshall felt like the entire rig was going to vibrate and disintegrate into pieces sinking right then and there.

"Get the BOP engaged!" Martinez screamed over and over, his voice barely audible over the chaos, and explosions. "Engage the damn BOP now!"

Despite the fact that his ears were ringing and he could not see very well, Marshall jumped to his feet and made a beeline for the controls. His fingers seemed to be dancing across the buttons as he frantically attempted to activate the Blowout Preventer. Then the oil company unit was the final line of defense standing between the men, the waters of the Gulf and a complete and utter catastrophe. After repeated attempts the Blowout Preventer system was still unresponsive, and the monitoring screens were flickering with error messages like some sort of video game. As the rig's functions struggled to keep up with the disaster that was taking place around them, both men came to the same realization... the worse had come and they needed to abandon the rig immediately.

"It's time to get the men moving to the lifeboats... we need to get off this damn rig!" Marshall said through clenched teeth, his hands trembling to the point of shaking as he attempted to engage the BOP for the 4th or 5th time. However, it was all of no use. The pressure from a mile under the water and the poorly maintained equipment were under an excessive amount of strain. They were running out of time with the rig continuing to lose the battle.

The acrid smell of smoke filled the air as the emergency alarms blared, their shrill wails echoing off the steel walls of the sinking rig. Martinez's heart pounded in his chest, his breath coming in ragged bursts as he ran down the narrow corridor. His boots thudded against the metal floor, each step vibrating through his legs. Overhead, red lights flashed and bathing the space in an eerie glow.

He rounded the corner, nearly colliding with Marshall, who was pulling on a breathing mask, his face already slick with sweat. The man's eyes were wide, his usual calm shattered.

"Marshall!" Martinez gasped, struggling to catch his breath. "Where do we go? How do we get the hell off this damn rig?"

Marshall didn't look up as he yanked the straps of his mask tight, his hands shaking slightly. "We head for the lifeboats. They're the only way off this thing in a fire. You remember where they are, right?"

Martinez's mind raced, trying to recall the layout of the rig. The drills, the safety briefings—it was all a blur now, drowned out by the roaring in his ears and the distant sound of something heavy crashing against the deck above.

"The aft side, right?" Martinez stammered. "By the supply cranes?"

Marshall nodded, his voice low but urgent. "Yeah, aft side. But we've got to get through the galley first, and with the fire spreading, it's gonna be a mess. The walkways are probably blocked by now."

Martinez's stomach clenched at the thought. The galley was three levels up, and the fire had started in the engine room—close to where they were now. If it spread further, there'd be no way through. He could already feel the heat intensifying, the thick smoke creeping into the air.

"Can't we head straight up to the deck from here?" Martinez asked, his voice rising in panic. "There's gotta be another way."

"There's no other way!" Marshall snapped, his eyes blazing through the visor of his mask. "The main stairwell's blocked—saw it myself. We have to go through the galley, or we're stuck down here. Unless you wanna take a dive into the ocean and hope you don't get roasted alive."

Martinez cursed under his breath, his hands trembling as he fumbled with his own mask. The thought of being trapped on the rig, surrounded by flames, was enough to make his legs weak. "What if we don't make it through?"

Marshall grabbed his arm, squeezing hard enough to snap Martinez's attention back to him. "We're gonna make it. But you need to keep your head on straight, you hear me? No panicking, no freezing up. We stick together, and we move fast. That's the only chance we've got."

Martinez nodded, swallowing hard. His throat felt dry, the taste of smoke bitter on his tongue. "Okay. We move fast," he said.

Marshall let go of his arm and gestured toward the ladder leading to the lower levels and the boats. "Follow me. Stay low, stay close. We get to the lifeboats… we're out of here."

Without waiting for a response, Marshall started climbing, his movements quick and efficient despite the chaos surrounding them. Martinez followed, the metal rungs cold under his hands as he hauled himself down. The heat grew more intense with every rung, the smell of burning plastic and metal growing stronger.

 They reached the lower inner are and needed to get to the outer level. Marshall pushed open the hatch to the galley. The instant the door swung open, a wave of blistering heat hit them full force, the air thick with smoke. Flames licked at the edges of the room, crawling up the walls and consuming everything in

their path. Tables were overturned, debris scattered everywhere. The wreckage was complete.

Marshall cursed under his breath. "Shit, it's even worse than I thought!"

Martinez hesitated, staring at the inferno before them. "How the hell are we supposed to get through that?" Between the flames and the smoke…
"We don't have a choice," Marshall said, his voice grim. "It's either this or we're trapped. Hug the walls, stay far from the flames… You got that?"

Martinez nodded, his mouth dry. "Yeah… I got it."

They crouched low and started moving, Marshall leading the way with deliberate, careful steps. The heat was suffocating, the smoke burning Martinez's lungs even through the mask. He could hear the fire crackling, roaring like some living beast as it tore through the galley. Every instinct screamed at him to turn back, but there was nowhere else to go. The rig was burning and sinking, and if they didn't make it to the lifeboats, they'd go down with it.

"Faster!" Marshall barked over the roar of the flames. "We're almost through!"

Martinez's legs ached, the heat making every movement feel like he was wading through thick mud. His vision blurred from the smoke, and his heart hammered in his chest. He could barely see Marshall in front of him now, just a shadow moving through the smokey haze. Finally, they reached the door on the far side of the galley. Marshall shoved it open, and they stumbled into the corridor beyond. The air was marginally clearer, but Martinez could still feel the heat pressing in from all sides. He ripped off his mask, gasping for breath.

"There," Marshall said, pointing down the corridor. "The lifeboats. We're almost home."

Martinez looked down the narrow hall, the flashing red lights and thick smoke making it hard to see. But at the end of the passage, through the haze, he could just make out the bright orange shapes of the lifeboats hanging from the side of the rig.

"We made it," Martinez breathed, half in disbelief.

"Not yet," Marshall said, his tone hard. "We've still gotta get those things in the water. Come on!"

They sprinted down the corridor, every step echoing off the metal walls. Behind them, the sound of the fire was growing louder, closer. They reached the lifeboats, and Marshall immediately started working the release mechanisms, his hands moving with practiced precision.

Martinez looked back toward the rig, watching as the flames consumed more of the structure, creeping ever closer to where they stood. "She's gonna goo down. Marshall, we need to go!"

"I'm working on it!" Marshall snapped, gritting his teeth as he pulled the lever. The lifeboat jolted, swinging slightly as the cables began to lower it precariously toward the ocean waves.

As the boat dipped toward the sea, Marshall grabbed Martinez's shoulder. "Get in! Now!"

They climbed into the lifeboat, the heat from the flames nearly unbearable now. The moment they were inside with 15 other crew mates, Marshall pulled the final release, and the boat plunged down toward the churning ocean below. For a moment, the world was nothing but fire and noise. Then, with a bone-rattling crash, they hit the water, the cold spray of the ocean engulfing them.

Martinez sat back, gasping for breath, his body shaking from the adrenaline. Marshall was beside him, breathing heavily but steady, his eyes fixed on the burning platform.

"Holy shit, we're alive," Martinez said, his voice barely a whisper.

Marshall nodded slowly, his gaze never leaving the flames. "Yeah. For now."

There was a spooky calmness in the sea, with its pitch-black surface reflecting the blazing sky above. Each swell of the waves seemed to be a shallow breath, as if the Gulf itself was holding back, waiting to see what would happen next. The lifeboat floated back and forth in the water. The acrid taste of smoke was still present in Marshall's mouth as he sat slumped against the side of the room. His chest was also heaving as he attempted to catch his breath.

The situation allowed no time to relax. The platform was burning—a raging inferno that reached up into the night, a beacon of disaster that would soon be known all over the world. The Deepwater Sky was burning and would do so for 24 hulls until it sank. The water echoed with the rig's groaning and cracking, the metal twisting and breaking. It was deteriorating, but it had not yet sunk.

"Where's the rest of the crew? Marshall was in a daze but Mercer's thin and wavering voice, broke through the din. Mercer was staring back at the rig the whole time, his eyes wide with terror. While the flames continued to dance in his vision, Marshall had to force himself to look. Flames were licking up the rig's sides now, and smoke was billowing into the sky like a storm. The rig had become a towering pyre. There was confusion about fire fighting boundaries. He could see figures running along the deck, small and frantic. Their movements desperate and erratic. Some were able to make it to the lifeboats, while others unfortunately, were not. They had trained for this… almost.

Marshall mumbled, "Jesus," while doing so under his breath. There were too many people still in the air, and a great number of them would not survive.

"They're trapped," Mercer murmured, his voice shaking slightly as he spoke. "They have no way of escaping now. Oh my god…"

Marshall was well aware that Mercer was correct. The fire had closed off the primary escape routes, and the secondary escape routes were rapidly approaching closure. While waiting for it to collapse, the flames consumed more of the rig. The anger that was rising in his chest fused with the fear and helplessness that had been engulfing him ever since the blowout. He clenched his fingers more tightly than ever before. His thoughts were racing as he looked for a solution, an answer, or anything else he could do to save those men. It was hopeless.

The voice of TJ reverberated in his head, reminding

him of a conversation that they had just a few days earlier. "They're going to burn," he said. "Just know that there's no going back if this all goes wrong,"

Immediately, Marshall pushed the thought out of his mind, and his instincts kicked in, compelling him to take action. The flickering flames illuminated Mercer's pale face as he looked at his. "Stay here," he said with a firm tone in his voice.

"What is it? Are you planning to go somewhere? His eyes widened with a look of panic.

Just as he was beginning to pull himself up, he announced, "I'm going back." Even though his body was begging for rest and his legs were shaking under him, he chose to ignore it. You are correct, Mercer; there are still people up there. I am obligated to assist them.

"Marshall, you can't!" Mercer reached out and grabbed his arm, and his hold was surprisingly firm. Don't do it. You're gonna die in there!"

The tone of his voice became more resolute as he moved away from his and said, "I'm not going to let those men burn, even if I'm only able to save one!"

"Marshall, can you please!" His eyes were pleading, and his voice was cracking. "You can't save them all. You'll simply die with them! We got to go now."

The pressure of his words was pressing down on

him, and he momentarily hesitated. But then he thought about the crew, the men he had worked alongside, the men he had shared meals with, joked with, and trusted with his life. He was unable to just leave them. Not now. Not ever.

As he spoke, his tone became more gentle but resolute. "I have got to try," he said.

The moment Mercer had the opportunity to stop him, Marshall climbed out of the lifeboat, his boots contacting the icy and slippery surface of the water. Despite the fact that the rig was still emitting heat, the water was extremely cold. This was a striking contrast. As he steadied himself, he wrapped his hands around the edge of the lifeboat and then turned his attention to the fire.

Despite the short distance to the rig, every inch was a battle. While he was swimming, the water rushed all around him, and the waves threatened to pull him down. His muscles were burning from the effort that he was putting forth. With every stroke, the heat became more intense, the flames crackled louder, and the roar of the fire was so loud that it drowned out everything else.

As soon as Marshall arrived at the bottom of the rig, he discovered a ladder with metal rungs that were scorching to the touch. He paused for a split second before beginning to climb, and then he continued climbing. Despite each rung feeling like it was searing his hands and the heat radiating through his gloves, he gritted his teeth and continued to climb.

As he continued to move, it seemed as though the smoke was wrapping itself around him like a shroud. Despite the fact that his lungs were struggling to cope with the toxic air, he continued to move forward. Every step was a struggle against the heat and smoke in the rig, which was ablaze with fire. Debris, including twisted metal, splintered wood, and the remnants of a structure once a symbol of human ingenuity, covered the deck he stood on.

"Please help me!" A weak and frantic voice emerged among all the chaos. Marshall's heart was pounding as he turned his attention toward the sound. Through the smoke, he was able to make out a figure clinging to a fallen piece of scaffolding. It turned out to be one of the roughnecks, with his face contorted in agony and his eyes wide from fierce fear.

"Hold on to it!" When Marshall was attempting to make his way through the debris, he yelled. To get closer to the man, he got down on his knees beside him. The scaffolding had crushed the roughneck's legs and he would be lucky to ever walk again.

The man sputtered, "Pppplease," his voice choking with smoke. "My legs... I... I'm unable to move."

As Marshall gripped the edge of the scaffolding, he urged the other person to have faith. "Y'all hang in there! We're going to get you out of here."

Despite the fact that his muscles were screaming in protest, he strained against the metal. The heat was intolerable, and the flames were getting closer, but he was unable to stop himself. With a final surge of strength, he lifted the scaffolding to the point where the roughneck was able to crawl out from under it.

"Make a move!" Marshall yelled out to the man, grabbed him by the arm, and pulled him to his feet. "You have to get moving!"

The roughneck was hobbled, his breath coming out in ragged gasps with each breath. They tried to make their way through the wreckage together, the fire raging around them all the while. However, Marshall continued to move forward, even though the intense heat felt like it was peeling off his face.

When they reached the deck's edge, he discovered that the lifeboats were still suspended just above the water. In the distance, Marshall could see the other members of the crew already loading into the boats; however, there was not much time left. The structure was groaning as it gave way to the flames, and the rig was falling under its own weight.

"Get going!" Marshall pushed the roughneck towards the nearest lifeboat and observed his descent down the ladder. While he was turning around to face the rig, his eyes were searching the deck for any indication of movement or life. But all he could see was flames.

Marshall paused for a brief period of time, feeling the pressure of the decision beginning to press down on him. The heat, the flames licking at his back, and the rig collapsing around him were all physical sensations that he could feel. There wasn't any time left. If he continued to stay, he would perish.

"Goddammit," he muttered as he turned around and ran in the direction of the ladder. As his hands searched for the rings, the burning sensation of the metal against his skin intensified. In spite of the fact that his heart was pounding in his chest, he crawled down, his feet slipping on the wet surface.

Immediately after he hit the water, the lifeboat

began to descend, with the remaining members of the crew already on board. In an effort to reach it, Marshall swam toward it, the icy water causing a shock to his system and his muscles shaking with exhaustion. Strong hands pulled him aboard the boat after it hit the water's surface, just in time.

Someone mumbled, "Jesus, Marshall," with a distinct tone of disbelief evident in their voice. "The damn boat might have hit you from way up there."

Marshall sputtered, "Yeah," he said as he began to collapse against the boat's side, his entire body trembling. "However, I ain't dead… not yet."

The flames continued to rise into the sky as the lifeboat moved away from the rig, but it continued to drift away. The image of the burning rig permanently scarred Marshall 's mind, despite the temperature dropping as they moved further out to sea. It was a vision of hell that would continue to torment him for the rest of his life.

The crew members sat in stunned silence, their faces covered in soot and fear, and their eyes reflecting the blaze from which they had just managed to free themselves. While Mercer was standing next to him, Mercer's hands were shaking as Mercer held on to the edge of the boat. With a mixture of relief and horror in his eyes, Mercer looked at him wide open.
In a barely audible whisper, Mercer said, "You made it," as the crackling flames made it difficult to hear. Although he was too exhausted to speak, Marshall

nodded. His entire body hurt, his lungs burned, and his mind was completely numb because of the shock. But they were still alive. They made it!

Marshall turned his head back for the final time as the lifeboat continued to drift further away from the rig. The Deepwater Sky, its bones consumed by fire and its structure disintegrating into the water, was a beast on its deathbed. They had no choice but to let the flames continue. The nightmare was not about to end it was just getting started.

As the blowout continued to intensify, the monstrous sound that seemed to originate from the very depths of the earth became even more audible. It sounded like a runaway freight train or a up close Jet Engine. Marshall and Martinez could now feel intolerable heat in the drilling control room. The heat was like a searing wave that rolled through and made it difficult to breathe. As he struggled to maintain his concentration and prevent his mind from slipping into a deeper state of panic, sweat began to pour down their faces. Following that, there was yet another explosion. Even larger this time, the blow up ripped through the rig, the shockwave destroying the drill control room, causing Marshall to crash into the wall and throwing Martinez out the missing monitor window that had overlooked the drill hole.

Occurring simultaneously there was a moment when the entire world turned white—a blinding flash of light and heat that robbed lungs of the air they'd been holding. The control room was in a state of destruction when Marshall's vision improved he could see that the monitors had been shattered, the consoles were sparking, debris was scattered everywhere and Martinez was nowhere to be found. He wondered to himself if he was gonna make it off the platform alive.

The ringing in Marshall's ears and the aching in his body caused him to struggle to get to his feet. To him it was so loud that he could hardly hear over the roar of the flames, but he didn't necessarily need to. He was aware of what was taking place. There was a fire on his rig and they needed to abandon the platform ASAP.

"Let's get the hell outta here!" Marshall yelled to anyone who'd listen. Using the rigs PA system, which miraculously was still functional, he put out one last order.

"Abandon the rig! Abandon rig! Abandon rig! Muster at your Lifeboat stations now..." the announcement on the platform was ominous.

Suddenly Martinez reappeared and grabbed by Marshall's arm pulling both men in the direction of the exit and the ladder down to the lifeboat stations. The moment that they emerged from the control room and made their way out onto the deck and night air, the pungent odor of burning oil assaulted their noses. Flames in the dark were now climbing the rig's sides and devouring everything in their path. The Gulf water itself was now on fire!

Marshall felt as though his skin was melting under the intense heat, which was all accompanied by a thick layer of smoke in the air. Suddenly, for some odd reason, he wondered if Mercer and the people from the Oil Company were still onboard and OK. Not that he really cared. After all he blamed them, at least in part for creating a culture of 'Go Fever' and throwing safety out the window. 'They made it all about profit and they got my men killed!' he thought to himself. 'And there's gonna be hell to pay, I'll see to it if it takes from here to forever.'

The faces of the crew members at their Muster stations were covered with expressions of fear, disbelief and confusion as they waited turns to disembark. The structure was being devoured by flames that crackled and hissed as the fire consumed the rig. It was now a war zone. Their minds a jumble of survival instincts and desperate plans, both men could hardly think in that state.

"Get on those life vests and get on the damn lifeboats now!" Marshall yelled as he pushed his way through the crowd, grabbing anyone who was within his reach, and pushing them toward potential escape routes to the lifeboats. "Move, move, move your ass,. let's goooooo! Fill them boats and no stragglers," he directed.

As the flames were getting closer, he was able to see some of the lifeboats were unfilled with crew and others were hanging precariously on the rig's edge. The heat was intolerable, and the flames were too close to load at least two of the boats. Marshall was now even more aware that they didn't have a lot of time left before the reached the point of no return.

Finally he caught a glimpse of wanna be oil man Daniel Mercer from corporate out of the corner of his eye. His once immaculate suit was now smeared with oil, grease and soot, his face pale with shock. Mercer was unable to fully comprehend what was taking place as he stood motionless in the midst of the chaos just staring at the fire.

"Mercer!" Marshall's voice became hoarse because of the smoke as he shouted, "See what happened you fool? Get on that damn Lifeboat right now!"

His eyes were wide but still unable to see very well. His hands were shaking as Mercer turned to face

97

A Lifeboat from the Deepwater Sky

him. Mercer appeared to be on the verge of collapsing for a brief period of time; however experiencing a moment of realization he promptly nodded and stumbled forward. They were making their way toward the lifeboats and it felt as though their shoes were being burned off by the intense heat of the metal deck. The state of the art rig was now just a labyrinth of twisted metal and flames. Despite his lack of clear sight, Marshall could hear the roar of the fire and the creaking of the rig's structure as it began to collapse under the strain. Both were totally audible to him despite his condition but after 15 years on the Deepwater Sky he could feel the destruction deep in his bones.

The moment they arrived at the lifeboats, the rig was rocked by another massive explosion, the force of which caused almost everyone to fall to the deck. Marshall's head slammed into the deck, and as he struggled to remain conscious, his vision began to blur even more and the ringing in his ears was now even louder than the fire around him. It was the sound of the rig tearing itself apart in a haze of smoke and flames. Surly this must be what hell is like, he thought

"Marshall!" When he heard Mercer's voice, it sounded faint and far away, as if Mercer were calling to him from the end of a very long tunnel. He was standing right next to him. Although he made an effort to respond, Marshall's mouth refused to cooperate, and his body was suddenly too weak to even move. Now Marshall realized that *he* was running out of time as total darkness encroached on his vision. While he struggled against it and attempted to claw his way back to consciousness, the pain and heat were too much for him to bear.

"Marshall!" After hearing Mercer's voice once more, this time with a greater volume, he felt hands on his shoulders shaking him and pulled him back from the edge of the deck. Marshall then made a tremendous effort to open his eyes, and as he did so, everyone and everything around him came back into focus. Mercer was hunched over him, his face covered in tears and soot, his expression one of complete and utter terror. In one look he let the rig boss know that he was sorry and that he understood Marshall was right about everything.

In a trembling voice, Mercer weirdly said, "Ummmmmm we have to leave now, Marshall, hope you don't mind."

"Hope you and the other company boys enjoyed the tour!" Marshall shot back sarcastically.

Despite the fact that his muscles were screaming in protest, he gave a feeble nod and struggled to get to his feet. The flames were getting ever closer as they made their way towards the lifeboats. If they didn't leave now they never would. With the metal groaning and twisting as the fire consumed it, they couldn't stop the rig's death. Not now.

After what seemed like an eternity, they arrived at the lifeboats, and Marshall almost pushed Mercer into one of them while his breath came out in ragged gasps. He turned his head to look back at the rig he loved and had spent more than 15 years working on. It was now a dreadful scene of destruction. Suddenly for a brief moment, he thought he saw young TJ Johnson, his silhouette framed by the flames on the far side of the platform and just as suddenly he disappeared. Before Marshall could react, the lifeboat was released, plunging them into the cool oil saturated waters below. Unable to do anything

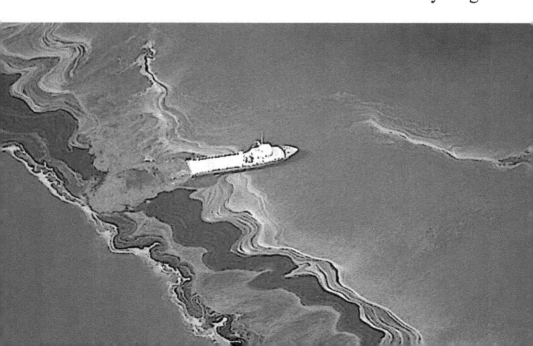

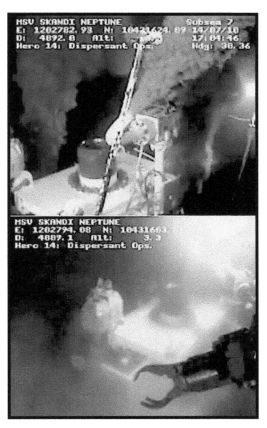

HSU SKANDI NEPTUNE   Subsea 7
E: 1202782.93 N: 10431624.09 14/07/10
D: 4892.8   Alt: 17:04:46
Hero 14: Dispersant Ops.   Hdg: 30.36

HSU SKANDI NEPTUNE
E: 1202794.08 N: 10431603.
D: 4889.1   Alt: 3.3
Hero 14: Dispersant Ops.

*Viewers could watch live
feeds of the well on TV*

further but flee, they watched as the rig slowly and agonizingly began the process of sinking (which would take almost 24 hours!). Looming above them like a burning monolith against the night sky the crew of the still couldn't believe it. Others wondered where the hell the United States Coast Guard was.

It was a combination of shock and cold that caused Marshall to collapse against the side of the lifeboat, his chest heaving and his body trembling. Mercer was standing next to him his sobs sharp and ragged. The Deepwater Sky, world's largest Oil Drilling Platform, was now taking up residence 5000' down on the floor of the Gulf. But that was just the beginning of the nightmare.

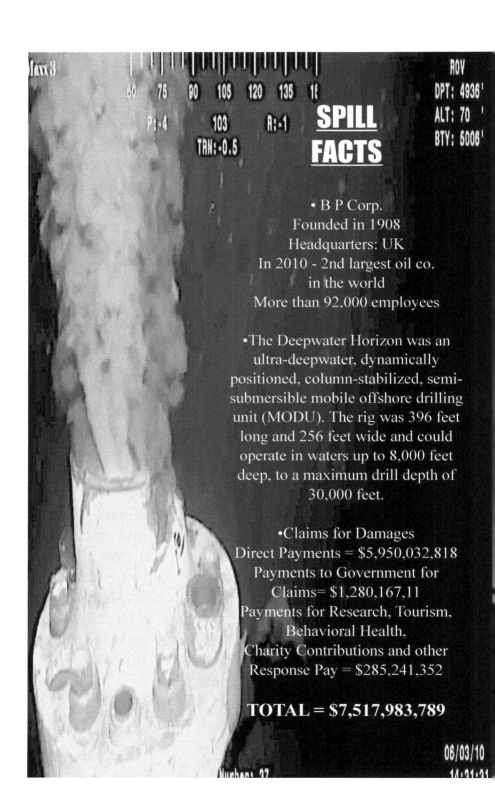

Maxx3
60 75 90 105 120 135 1b
P:-4 103 R:-1
TRN:-0.5

ROV
DPT: 4936'
ALT: 70 '
BTY: 5006'

SPILL
FACTS

• B P Corp.
Founded in 1908
Headquarters: UK
In 2010 - 2nd largest oil co.
in the world
More than 92,000 employees

•The Deepwater Horizon was an
ultra-deepwater, dynamically
positioned, column-stabilized, semi-
submersible mobile offshore drilling
unit (MODU). The rig was 396 feet
long and 256 feet wide and could
operate in waters up to 8,000 feet
deep, to a maximum drill depth of
30,000 feet.

•Claims for Damages
Direct Payments = $5,950,032,818
Payments to Government for
Claims= $1,280,167,11
Payments for Research, Tourism,
Behavioral Health,
Charity Contributions and other
Response Pay = $285,241,352

TOTAL = $7,517,983,789

06/03/10
14:31:31
Number: 27

Chapter 6

A Gulf of Oil
Hiding Millions of Gallons of Crude

The sun rose over the Gulf of Mexico, casting long shadows across the placid waters and staining the horizon with lingering traces of smoke. As dawn broke, the Deepwater Sky was nothing more than a smoldering wreck, its skeletal remains protruding out of the water like the bones of some fallen giant. The inferno had burned through the night, but now, as dawn broke, the Deepwater Sky was nothing more than a heap of metal in the water.

Marshall sat on the deck of the Coast Guard cutter, his back pressed against the cold metal railing, his eyes fixed on the horizon. Despite the fact that he'd not slept two days —none of them had—he was too numb and tired to feel anything that could be considered exhaustion. After a long period of time, the adrenaline that had kept him going throughout the night had worn off, leaving him with a void that tore at him from the inside out.

The crew was in shock with 11 confirmed missing. Their voices were low, and their eyes were hollow as they huddled together in small clusters. Some of them appeared to be trying to make sense of the nightmare that they had just survived by staring out at the water, whereas others were just gazing down at the deck with a blank look of disbelief. There was a still strong odor of smoke and oil in the air, a stench that clung to their clothing, their skin, their hair and now their memories. The smell was everywhere and would prove to be unforgettable.

It appeared as though Mercer was attempting to keep himself together as he sat silently next to Marshall with his knees drawn up to his chest and his arms wrapped around them. If he could curl up in the fatal position he would have done so. Since they had been pulled from the lifeboat, Mercer had not spoken a single word to anyone. His face pale and his eyes just red rims in response to the smoke and tears. Marshall could see that Mercer was reliving it over and over in his mind. The shock had settled over him like a heavy fog, and Mercer was still trapped in the inferno.

"Hey," Marshall said in a low voice, his voice rough from the smoke he had been inhaling. Stumped for words, he couldn't stand the silence any longer. "We have succeeded… the system worked and you're safe," he said softly.

There was no response from Mercer, he didn't even look up. The Moon, reaching higher altitudes and painting the sky with various shades of red and orange, riveted his attention on the horizon in the far distance. Even though the moon rise over the Gulf was beautiful, it didn't hold any beauty for him. Not right now. Like most of the crew he was in a state of shock and it was at times like these that he wondered if he was just an insane roughneck.

Marshall let out a sigh as he ran his hand through his densely matted hair. He experienced a sense of disconnection, as if the world around him was moving at a glacial pace, and he was merely playing the role of a spectator, observing everything unfold from a distance. The fire had destroyed his rig, but the realization of what had happened and the lives lost was just beginning to fully sink in.

He repeated, this time more to himself than anyone, "We're alive," and he said it once more. "We are alive!" Even though it was an undeniable and unambiguous fact, it did not bring him the relief he had expected or hoped. The magnitude of the loss overshadowed any victory of living thru it.

The rescue boat's engines rumbled away beneath them, producing a low, consistent hum that reverberated throughout the deck as they made their way back to shore. Soon they would be disembarking from the boat and to Marshall, Martinez and the crew it felt like they were returning from another planet where reality no longer applied. During the trip back most of them swore, at least to themselves, that they'd never drill for oil ever again.

As Marshall's thoughts wandered, he found himself thinking about the men they had lost, the faces he would never see again… the voices that the fire had permanently silenced. He had a mental image of one of his favorite roughnecks, TJ, smiling at him from across the mess hall table. A cigarette dangled from his lips, and his laughter piercing the din of clattering plates and silverware. TJ was filled with energy and confidence firmly believing in his invincibility. He was on the missing list.

Marshall mumbled, "I should have done more," as the guilt tightened its hold on his heart and mind. "I *could* have done more," he said. It was as if his mind was filled with what-if scenarios, each one more debilitating than the one before it. But what if he'd taken action earlier? Imagine, for a moment, that he had noticed the signs earlier. What if he had been more intelligent, more powerful, and faster? Then perhaps all of them would be present and headed home… and TJ wouldn't be just a memory.

"Marshall?" Even though Mercer's voice was soft, it penetrated the fog that was present in his mind like a knife. He turned to face him, surprised to see his eyes filled with something he could not precisely identify. "You succeeded in every way that you could out here. We were all there and a whole lot more folks could have died. I know that," he said. 'The company needs to understand and be held accountable. For my part I am sorry," he said.

Although Marshall wanted to argue with him and tell Mercer that there was always something else that they could have done, but the words were unable to come out. And besides Mercer was absolutely correct. They had fought with everything they had, but unfortunately, it had not been enough to save the rig. Both men understood that they would have to bear the burden of guilt the rest of their lives. It was not an easy task.

"Yeah," he finally said, his voice thick with the emotion he was feeling.

Mercer gave a slight, melancholy nod for a moment. But in his heart he didn't feel like this was the case.

With the tragedy hanging between them, they fell silent again. While treating their visible and invisible wounds, the crew moved like ghosts. Their movements were slow and deliberate but they were effective. The medics moved among them, providing blankets, water, and words of comfort; however, the emotionless expressions on the survivors' faces revealed that bandages could not contain the grief they were experiencing.

Marshall, having removed one of the roughnecks from the rig, sat with his head in his hands, his shoulders trembling with silent sobs. Marshall watched as this occurred. He wanted to go to him in order to provide him with some form of solace, but he was at a loss for exactly what to say. How would you respond to a man who had just witnessed the destruction of his entire world?

The sound of helicopters approaching from the distance caught Marshall 's attention. When he looked up, he saw a long line of helicopters flying through the sky, their rotors slicing through the air as the morning air passed by. Even though they were search and rescue personnel, their sight did not provide any comfort because of the stark contrast between their bright colors and the pale sky. Their arrival was too late.

During the descent of the helicopters, Marshall's thoughts turned to the days that were still to come. News crews, eager to dissect the tragedy for the evening broadcasts, would swarm like vultures, conducting investigations and interviews. People from all over the world would seek answers, looking to men like Marshall to provide information. So what could he possibly say? When it came to those last moments on the rig, how could he possibly explain the chaos, fear, and helplessnesst he felt?

As soon as the helicopters touched down on the deck, the crew of the cutter immediately went into action. The cutter's blades created a strong wind that tore at their clothing and sent loose debris skittering across the metal surface. Medical personnel emerged from the helicopters, their expressions gloomy and their movements swift as they began to evaluate the individuals who had survived.

As the medical personnel approached, Marshall observed them, but he experienced a sense of disconnection, as if he were watching a scene from a movie. With his mind still engulfed in the blaze, he instinctively responded when one of them kneeled in front of him and inquired about his injuries. These questions were about his injuries.

During the time that Mercer was wrapping a blanket around his shoulders, the medical professional gave him a tight smile and assured him that everything would be okay. "We are going to get you all back home," Mercer said.

It's home. It was a concept that seemed far away and unreal to Marshall , and the word sounded quite foreign to him. What could he consider home now that the rig was no longer there? Over the previous year, he had dedicated more time to his work on the Deepwater Sky than he had to his own apartment. The rig, once his home and world, had now crumbled to ash and twisted metal.

He accepted the words of the medic with a numb nod, but there was a hollowness in his ears as he listened to them. You should feel complete and secure at home. It was supposed to be a place where you could unwind and relax. After everything that had transpired and the things that he had witnessed, Marshall was unsure that he would ever feel complete again. It was a life altering event to him.

The helicopters took off again, bringing with them some of the crew members who had suffered more serious injuries, leaving the cutter to continue its journey back to shore. As Marshall watched them vanish into the horizon, their shapes steadily shrank until they were nothing more than specks on the horizon.

In a low voice, Mercer addressed him as "Marshall ," thereby refocusing his attention on him. "Everything is going to turn out for the best. Despite the fact that it's going to be difficult, we'll prevail," he said. "Besides there's more than enough blame to go around and I'm sure everyone will get their due lashes when it is all said and done."

It was difficult for Marshall to believe him and cling to the hope that Mercer was offering. He wanted to believe him but he knew Mercer very well and was said out here was not the same thing said at oil command headquarters. His mind etched the images of the rig catching fire and the men trapped in the flames, unable to shake the feeling that they had only just begun to deal with the consequences of what had occurred. There was still an uncapped well head down there spewing thousands of gallons of crude into the Gulf every day.

He responded with a "yes," despite the fact that the word was cumbersome to him. The phrase 'We'll get through it' was disingenuous at best. Marshall knew nothing would ever be the same and that somehow the crew and TransSea would get the lions share of the blame. The fire had left its mark on all of them, scars that would never fully heal, despite the fact that they had survived the devastating blaze. The destruction of multi billion dollar Deepwater Sky was a catastrophe that would remain a part of their memories wherever they went...forever.

While the ship continued its journey toward TransSea's port in Louisiana, Marshall closed his eyes in an effort to block out the images that were tormenting him like the raging inferno that just a few hours earlier refused to be silent.

As the shore got closer one of the people from the corporate visitors moved through the crew asking them not to speak with the press on the pier. Two things were now clear to Marshall (and back at HQ, the rig's owner TransSea Corp.), one, was that the Deepwater Sky was a total loss and secondly that the most difficult part was yet to come. He came to realize that even if they had extinguished the flames, the aftermath would persist, forcing them to try reconstructing a life irreparably shattered by the events of the past 48 hours. And then there was the uncapped oil well at the bottom of the Gulf.

Chapter 7

A Black Tide
Catastrophe on the Water

For centuries the horizon of the Gulf had always been a clear straight line, a distinct boundary that separated the boundless blue of the Gulf of Mexico from the boundless expanse of the sky. However, after 75 years that line had become dotted with thousands of drilling platforms and oil pumping stations, a skyline smudged with a black haze. There was now a thick, suffocating, and nauseating odor that clung to everything, and the sea had become dangerous. It was a vast, oily wasteland that stretched as far as the eye could see.

Marshall stood on the dock's edge, gazing out at the destruction. The oil was everywhere. It was a sickening reminder of what had been let loose, and what was still happening in the Gulf 5000' down. The wind blew softly, carrying with it the foul odor of crude oil mixed with the salty tang of the ocean. There were dark streaks of oil spreading out like veins in a dying body, and the waters, which had been pristine in the past, had become tainted. It was not blue-green anymore... it was grey or worse yet... black and it was literally everywhere.

It wasn't the first time Marshall had witnessed oil spills; they were relatively minor accidents that were quickly contained and cleaned up. However, this incident was completely unique. The magnitude was staggering, and the amount of oil involved was extremely high. It covered everything that was in its way, suffocating the water and transforming the waves into a slow, viscous sludge. It destroyed everything that was in its way.

Mercer remained silent beside him, his arms tightly wrapped around herself as if Mercer were attempting to protect herself from the terrifying scene that was unfolding in front of them. His face was pale, a look of disbelief in his eyes. Mercer had been with Marshall and Martinez on the rig, witnessing the fire and the destruction up close and personal. Now a different kind of nightmare was unfolding… slowly and inexorably, with no end in sight. The well was spewing thousands of gallons of raw oil into the Gulf of Mexico every hour of every day and no one outside of the Gulf seemed to care.

Mercer murmured, "They said it would be this bad," his voice barely audible over the soft lapping of the waves against the dock. "They said it would be bad," he repeated. "I had no idea. Oh my god," he said hanging his head.

Marshall didn't respond. Words could not adequately convey the magnitude of the catastrophe they were witnessing, and nothing he said could ameliorate or moderate their feelings about the situation. Despite the destruction of the Deepwater Sky, its legacy loomed before them, a sea of oil that would haunt them for years to come. It was bad enough to lose the multimillion dollar rig but the very Gulf itself was threatened. And worse yet from the Oil company to the government no body seems to understand the gravity of the situation and the response was slow if at all.

The crew on board a small boat floating in the nearby water was moving slowly and methodically as they attempted to deploy containment booms. Somehow, oil had stained the boat's hull. The efforts at containment were fruitless, like putting a band-aid on a bleeding wound that was gushing out of control. The oil spill was too extensive and persistent but it was feeding a media monster with live video from the air or of the wellhead deep underwater on the 'Moon'. Must watch TV!

It was like trying to fight back an ocean with a bucket. Marshall could see other boats in the distance with more crews working to stem the black tide. Meanwhile he started seeing large planes fly over. The Gulf had turned into a battlefield, and despite efforts anyone who cared about the Gulf was suffering a devastating loss.

A brown pelican floated by, its wings weighed down by oil; the once-majestic bird had become a pitiful and struggling creature after its transformation. Marshall watched the creature struggle to pull itself out of the water by flapping its wings weakly, but it was unsuccessful. After a few unsuccessful attempts, the bird finally gave up, its head drooping in exhaustion. The oil had adhered to the feathers,

making it heavier to heavy to fly or even move. As one of the many victims, it was a small part of the ecological disaster unfolding live on cable TV.

"I don't know how we're going to fix this," Mercer said, his voice shaking with the weight of the truth. "It's not going to be enough is it?"

Marshal felt the frustration, anger and helplessness rising up inside of him again, and he clenched his fists in response. They had worked to put out the fire and managed to survive the destruction of the rig, but this was something that they were unable to fight. They were powerless to stop the oil from spreading, which was like a black tide moving further and more quickly than anyone anticipated.

"We'll do what we can, but you get on the phone and tell HQ to get off their asses and help!" Marshall said. He knew it wouldn't be enough, and no matter how hard they tried, they couldn't and wouldn't reverse the damage. However, he understood that they couldn't simply abandon the Gulf of Mexico and let the oil leak from the deep-sea well forever.

As the sun rose higher in the sky, its rays reflected off of the oily water, transforming the surface into a mirror that was smooth and shimmering. Even though the 95 degree heat was unbearable and the humidity was encircling them like a wet blanket, but Marshall barely seemed to notice either of these things. He was consumed by the realization that they were facing a catastrophe that would redefine their lives for years to come. He imagined not being able to swim or fish the Gulf anymore. He was sad, angry and determined all at the same time. The magnitude of the task ahead consumed his mind.

As they prepared to go out onto the water, a group of men dressed in Hazmat suits appeared on the TransSea dock. Masks covered their faces, and their movements were deliberate and precise. They were a small team among many others that were participating in the cleanup efforts. However, as Marshall watched them, he couldn't help but feel that the entirety of the endeavor was pointless. It was becoming increasingly difficult to contain the oil with each passing hour damage was increasing, compounding, and spiraling out of control. The oil was spreading faster than efforts could contain it. The words "Mr. Marshall " came out of Mercer's mouth, and his voice penetrated Marshall's thoughts. Mercer extended his hand and touched his arm, thereby bringing him back to the present moment. "It's imperative that we get off this rig!"

He nodded and averted his stair once more, drawing his eyes away from the water and the nightmare unfolding before him. He was aware that Mercer was correct; there was nothing else that they could do right now. However, before he left, Marshall glanced at the horizon, focusing on the dark line that marked the boundary between the past, present and the dark future of the Gulf he loves.

The sea was being transformed into a cemetery, a final resting place for dreams, lives, and a future marred by greed and carelessness. In addition, as Marshall walked away, he was aware that even if it stopped now, the oil would leave its mark. And that was regardless of how hard they fought and how much effort they put into cleaning it all up. And that was the point. It would be a stain that never completely disappeared, serving as a constant reminder of the consequences of a company's greed and lack of being prepared.

The disaster they were leaving behind would continue as they returned to the H2 Hummer that gets 12 miles per-gallon. As they made their way, the sound of waves lapping against the oil-soaked dock followed them. It was nice weather but the

sunshine did not succeed in dispelling the darkness that had placed itself over Marshall's heart.

The road stretched out in front of them, leading them away from the coast and away from the sea of oil that had once been the Gulf of Mexico. As they traveled, they drove in silence. But no matter how far they traveled, Marshall knew the images would stay with him, etched into his memory like scars. Future efforts may clean up the oil, restore the beaches, and rehabilitate the wildlife, but the real and long-lasting damage had already been done and Marshall knew it was irreversible.

The Oil Company tried to cover things up. Press photographers were granted access only with company officials escorting them. In one example, the U.S. Coast Guard stopped Jean-Michel Cousteau's boat and allowed it to proceed only after the Coast Guard was assured that no journalists were on board. In another example, a CBS News crew was denied access to the oil-covered beaches of the spill area and when stopped from filming was told by authorities, "It's Oil Company's rules, not ours!"

The black tide that was swallowing the sea had tainted everyone's future. As the two men continued their journey, Marshall asked himself why he was in a car with a man be basically despised and blamed at least in part, for the spill. It was bizarre.

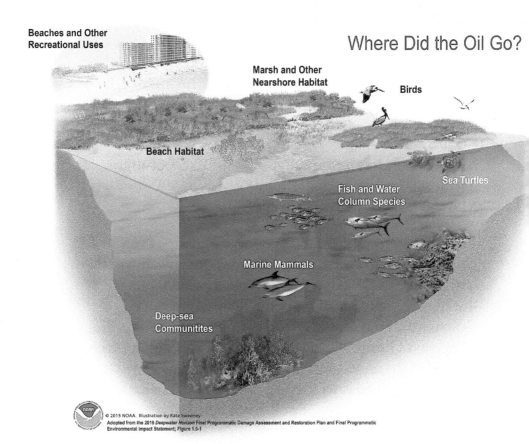

Where Did the Oil Go?

Beaches and Other Recreational Uses

Marsh and Other Nearshore Habitat

Birds

Beach Habitat

Sea Turtles

Fish and Water Column Species

Marine Mammals

Deep-sea Communitites

© 2015 NOAA. Illustration by Kate Sweeney
Adopted from the 2016 *Deepwater Horizon* Final Programmatic Damage Assessment and Restoration Plan and Final Programmatic
Environmental Impact Statement; Figure 1.5-1

Chapter 8

The Investigation
Everybody's Guilty and Nobody Is

When compared to the disorder that prevailed on the rig that night, the conference room at Oil Company headquarters in Houston was a striking contrast. The polished mahogany table, the neatly arranged chairs, and the crisp suits of the men and women gathered around it demonstrated the place's vibe and organization, with nothing out of place. However, beneath the surface, the tension was palpable, akin to a coiled spring ready to snap.

The corporation let him go a week after the 'incident' in the Spring of 2010 by Fall Jason Marshall, former Rig Boss on the Deepwater Sky was sitting at the opposite end of the table, his back straight and his hands tightly clasped in his lap sitting across from a dozen lawyers. Soot-stained work clothes and boots made him look out of place among the executives and lawyers aka 'The Suits'. His boots and work clothes served as a stark reminder of his background. Compared to the pungent odor of oil and smoke that was still present in his nostrils from 12 weeks ago... now the air was thick with the aroma of expensive cologne and gourmet coffee.

When Deepwater Sky was still just a dream, a project that was discussed over polished PowerPoint presentations and blueprints, he'd been in this room before and from a political standpoint he had been in this position before too. But the atmosphere in the room had definitely changed; it was chillier and much more hostile. It appeared as though everyone at the table was attempting to avoid drawing attention to themselves, as evidenced by the grim expressions on their faces and the hushed voices.

The door at the far end of the room opened, revealing a tall thin man in a dark suit. His presence immediately commanded attention from everyone in the room. He was one of the most senior executives at the Oil Company, and his reputation preceded him. His name was David Sterling. He had a reputation for having a sharp mind and an even sharper tongue. He was a man who could quickly cut any BS and excuses with a single glance.

"Let's begin," Sterling said with a serious tone in his voice, as he took his seat at the head of the table. The pleasantries and idle chatter were not something that he bothered with or wasted time with. He showed up in search of answers.

"This is not a hearing in a court of law but by the time the Texas sun goes down today two things are gonna be true… One is that Corporate is gonna know what in the sam hell went on out there… and the other is… I'm gonna have somebody's ass in my briefcase!" Sterling said. The room was stone silent. The pressure of the impending questions was pressing on Marshall mind like a vise, his heart pounding in his chest. Over the past few days, he had spent his time talking with his Attorney and mentally reliving the events that had transpired that night. He was looking for anything that he could have done differently—anything that could have prevented the catastrophe from occurring. He could find nothing in his mind nor in the records from the rig nor in his heart that would allow him to come to any other conclusion. On the other hand, the more he pondered the matter, the more he was unable to find the answers or second guess the decisions he and his team made that day.

Sterling opened a thick 6" folder in front of him and quickly flipped through the pages of the documents with the efficiency of a pro. He started by saying, "We're here to determine the cause of the blowout and to fully understand what went wrong. And why our company loss a rig worth more than $350 million." His eyes were searching the room as he introduced himself.

The others mumbled in agreement, but none of them looked towards Marshall. But he was able to look into their eyes and see the fear that they were experiencing—it was a different fear than the one that night. This was a fear that they would be the ones who had to take the blame and take responsibility for the disaster. The situation threatened livelihoods, careers, reputations, and billions of dollars in damages. Everyone in this room understood the stakes.

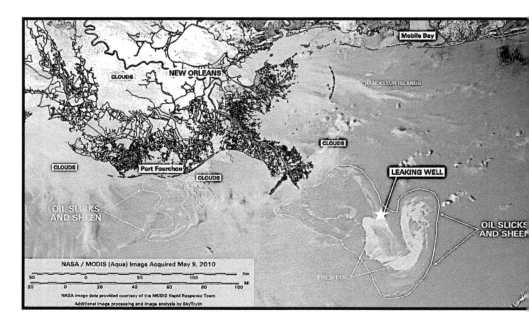

NASA / MODIS (Aqua) Image Acquired May 9, 2010

NASA image data provided courtesy of the MODIS Rapid Response Team
Additional image processing and image analysis by SkyTruth

Next the name "Mr. Jason Marshall, TransSea Incorporated," came out of Sterling's mouth as he looked up from his papers and focused his attention on him for the first time. "You were the Rig Supervision of the Deepwater Sky the night of the incident is that correct?

"Yes sir," responded Marshall.

"How long have you been with the company?" Sterling asked. Marshall found it very interesting but not surprising that company man Mercer was no where to be seen.

"Oh I don't work for the oil company, as you well know, I work for, or I had worked for TransSea who owned the Deepwater Sky and I have worked for them for 18 years with 15 years on the Sky. I was with her since she was born," Marshall said proudly.

"Like your job?" Sterling asked.

"I did... loved it." Marshall said the bitterness in his voice easy to hear.
"Mr. Marshall could you please provide us with a detailed account of the events that transpired that night," Sterling asked.

Marshall was feeling the weight of every eye in the room upon him, he took a deep breath. Despite his palms sweating and his throat being dry, he forced himself to speak.

"The pressure test was the first problem," he began, maintaining a steady and calm tone in his voice. "During our inspection of the well, we made certain that everything was in a stable state. But on hindsight the readings were not accurate; there was a problem... with something."

Sterling nodded slightly, his expression uncharitable, "Please Mr. Marshall go on..."

Marshall took a deep breath as he attempted to organize his thoughts and keep them in order. "Despite the fact that we reported the anomaly, orders were given to proceed with doing the pull and leaving for the next drill site. They told us that the reading was erroneous and that the well was in excellent condition. As a result, we continued with operations," Marshall explained.

"Two questions Sir..." Sterling said. "When you

first got back on the rig earlier that day who exactly told you things were... fine? I mean who specifically? I don't mean to put you on the spot..."

"Of course you do! The guys the company, your company brought in, your engineers, that's who told us everything was OK and the cement was a go. And to be clear sir, these were definitely not TransSea people," Marshall said.

Since the 'accident' when Marshall spoke, his voice was always barely audible just above a whisper. "And then the blowout happened," he continued. "We didn't have enough time to respond because the pressure was building up so quickly. After gas started shooting up the riser, the rig caught fire before we fully realized what was happening and could stop it. It was totally out of control!"

"Were you?" asked Sterling.

"No sir!" said Marshall incredulously. "We dealt with what Mother Nature gave us. We did it by the book and what my 18 years out there dictated.

Looking back I would not have changed a thing. It's easy to sit in an air condition office and criticize!"

"Your decisions cost the lives of 11 fine men sir!" Sterling said sternly the tension increasing 10 fold.

"How dare you sir! It was not *my* decisions it was *yours*!!" Marshall said almost shouting. "Corporate pushed us to the point of... destruction. And if you want see it the result of your go fever lies 50 miles out and one mile down on the bottom of the Gulf!"

Sterling and the room was in utter silence, and the weight of his words descended upon the atmosphere like an angry cloud. The other men at the table were visibly uncomfortable shifting in their seats as the realization of the truth began to sink in. Marshall could see this happening and so could Martinez who was now sitting 2 rows back.

"This was not merely an equipment malfunction or human error, was it? Rather, it was a catastrophic failure of both, and it killed and ruin people's lives,' Marshall concluded with sad tone.

While he was thinking about what Marshall had said, Sterling leaned back in his chair and knitted his fingers together. "Mr. Marshall, are you implying that someone in a higher managerial position made the decision that led to the blowout?" He said it in a way that told you he had already made up his mind what the answer would and should be.

The question hung in the air like a loaded gun. Marshall hesitated before answering it. Basically Sterling was asking him whether he was willing to point the finger at Oil Corporation management and place the blame at the feet of the individuals who had given the orders. He was completely aware of what Sterling was really asking. Answering truthfully was a risky, particularly because it had the potential to cost him everything. He would never work in the oil business ever again.

Meanwhile as he sat there, Marshall re-saw the faces of the men who had died on the burning rig that night. He knew that he couldn't lie… they would turn in their graves if he did.

Finally, he responded, "Yes," he said firmly and matter of factly. "We were following the oil company's instructions and despite our efforts to report and then fully investigate these problems… we received instructions to proceed with all due haste and that direction came from the Oil company not TransSea!" Marshall said emphatically.

The tension in the room increased by several notches as murmurs spread throughout the large conference room. The pupils in Sterling's eyes contracted, and his gaze became even more icy. "And Mr. Marshall, who was the person who issued those orders?" Sterling asked.

Despite the fact that Marshall's heart was pounding in his chest, he did not waver. "The TransSea office

in Louisiana confirmed that they received the orders, sir. It was someone in a position of authority at your firm, but I'm not entirely sure who gave the final go. Mr Mercer was your senior company man on site… but I noticed he is not here," Marshall said.

A darkening of Sterling's expression occurred, and his lips pressed together to form a tight thin line. There was a clear indication that his mind was working through the implications of Marshall 's statement. He did not immediately respond. After a long silence, he finally spoke, his tone was icy , determined and matter of fact…

"Mr. Marshall, Thank you very much, we'll take all his into consideration" Sterling said.

Marshall gave a slight nod, and he was aware of the shift that was taking place in the room, as well as the sudden change in his mood. He had just implicated the very individuals seated at this table, and he knew full well that he would face consequences for his actions and for laying the blame where it belongs. On the other hand, as he leaned back in his chair, he experienced a real sense of relief. Speaking truth was the only thing he could do.

From that point on, the rest of the meeting was a whirlwind of accusatory questions and cover your ass answers, with technical jargon flying over Marshall's head as the engineers (and the lawyers) dissected every aspect of the disaster and his response to it. There was animated discussion regarding the cementing process, the weight and pressure differentials of the mud, and safety protocols that had been neglected or disregarded prior to this point. On the other hand, Marshall was able to sense the underlying current of blame and the unspoken accusation that lingered in the air throughout the entire 2 hour discussion. The Oil Company had every intention on pinning any blame directly on TransSea and by extension Marshall.

When the meeting adjourned, Marshall and Martinez were the first to leave the room. As they walkedThe weight of the judgment that was to come would be significant. But Marshall maintained his composure and kept his shoulders square, resolute to conceal the fact that he was becoming increasingly distressed. Martinez said little and was not the gregarious man from a year ago. He shook Marshall's hand gave him a 'man hug' and walked away. Marshall never saw or heard from him again.

As the fluorescent lights buzzed overhead in the

hallway, casting harsh shadows on the room's pale blue walls. The sound of Marshall's footsteps reverberated through the empty corridor as he continued his journey to the elevator. However, despite feeling exhausted, as if his life had been sucked out of him, he also experienced a peculiar sense of calmness that settled over him. After he had confronted the flames and spoken the truth to the powers that be, he was now prepared to deal with whatever was next. Now he was ready to heal.

Marshall entered the elevator and pressed the button that led to the lobby, as the elevator doors slid open by themselves he glimpsed his reflection in the polished steel as the doors closed. The memories of that night haunted his gaunt and pale face. His appearance suggested that he had gone through hell, and in many respects, he had. And he was alone. His wife, unable to take the stress, had left and gone to her Mother's a month ago.

While the ride down was slow and each floor passed by with a gentle ding, Marshall hardly noticed the slowness of the ride. He was already thinking about what was going to happen next, including the media, the lawsuits, and the never-ending questions. His mind was already racing ahead. He knew that the investigation was far from complete and that the worst was yet to come.

After what seemed like an eternity, the elevator finally arrived at the lobby, and Marshall stepped out into the bustling atrium. The noise and movement of the city outside provided a striking contrast to the silence that the conference room had been experiencing. With his eyes darting in response to the sudden illumination, he made his way through the glass doors out into the bright Texas sunshine.

The throng of media and rig workers was massive and while standing on the sidewalk, the heat from the pavement was rising in waves. He took a deep breath and attempted to clear his mind as he stood there, he understood he was no longer able to control the situation. "Thank you!" "Right on man..." "Tell it!" calls came from the gathered crowd. Marshall was unable to shake the feeling that he was nothing more than a small cog in a much larger machine now—one that was completely beyond his ability to influence let alone control.

Although the investigation would continue for years, Marshall knew he'd already completed the most difficult part of the process. He had confronted the truth, and now he would face the consequences of his actions. He would never work in the profession he loved ever again. However, as he made his way away from the Oil company's plush headquarters, his steps were heavy, and his thoughts were already returning to the rig. He couldn't help but wonder if the truth would be sufficient to put things back in order. Or had it already been much too late? He got into his F-250 truck and drove away.

Chapter 9

Snakes in Suits
Playin the Blame Game

This was the kind of tension that made the air thicker and harder to breathe. The room was buzzing with tension. The fluorescent lights illuminated the room, pressing everyone's faces together and clenching their jaws in anticipation of the inevitable confrontation. There were rows upon rows of industry suits, government officials, and lawyers, each one more polished than the one before it. Marshall sat near the back of the room, his eyes scanning the rows. Everyone knew that the stakes had never been higher. Someone had to shoulder all the blame and now former Rig Boss Jason Marshall felt like it was gonna be him for sure!

At the front of the room was a long wooden table seated a group of senators. Their expressions were as stony and unreadable. They carefully positioned the microphones in front of them like weapons, ready to record every word and every mistake. With the composure of a man who had been well-prepared for combat, David Sterling, the top executive at the oil company, sat at a table on one side in the middle of everything. Marshall and other TransSea people sat in the first row. He noticed that Mercer was again missing in action and no where to be seen. Despite his unflinching demeanor and impeccable tailored suit, there was a sharpness to Sterling's eyes, indicating he was prepared to deflect, pivot, defend and otherwise survive. After all hearings were nothing new to him or the corporation. They basically live in court.

On the other side of Sterling and company, the attorneys representing TranSea, and the various other contractors involved in the Deepwater Sky project were rummaging through their notes. Documents and strategies filled their briefcases. The delicate nature of the dance created a legal minefield where a single mistake could cost millions bring everything crashing down.

As Marshall watched everything unfold, he did so with a mixture of fear and disinterest. Despite the fact that he'd been a participant in this catastrophe, it seemed far away and almost unreal to him here in this room. Words on paper, arguments in a courtroom, and a never ending game of shifting blame were reducing the oil, the fire, and the deaths to mere abstractions. It somehow all seemed unconnected to the actual suffering occurring in and around the Gulf coast.

The gavel banged. "The committee will come to order! We will now hear testimony from Mr. David Sterling of Oil Corporation," announced one of the Senators, his voice loud enough to overpower the ongoing conversations in the hearing room. Sterling, who had no trouble rising from his seat and approaching the microphone, became the focus of everyone's attention. He was sworn in.

With a steady and authoritative tone, Sterling began by expressing his gratitude to the Senators. He took a quick look around the room, his eyes moving over the number of people who had gathered. First and foremost, I would like to convey the most sincere condolences of Oil Corporation to the families of the fallen rig workers and for the unfortunate events that took place on the Deepwater Sky in April of 2010. Both the deaths and the environmental damage are tragedies affecting everyone here," he said.

As a result of Sterling's deliberate word choice, Marshall experienced another brief moment of anger. I am sorry. It is a tragedy! He thought to himself. These were nothing more than empty phrases, meaningless platitudes that did nothing to address or get the bottom of the actual problem. Although Marshall knew he shouldn't have expected more from the him he was disappointed but not surprised. Sterling was not present to provide answers or solutions; rather, he was present to safeguard his company and deflect responsibility whenever possible.

As one of the Senators leaned forward a little bit, his eyes narrowed. "Mr. Sterling, could you kindly clarify the reason for disregarding the well's pressure tests? What was the rationale behind the decision to move forward in spite of the obvious indications of instability with the well?"

Sterling, unfazed, didn't flinch. "We made the decision to proceed, Senator, based on the available information at the time. We examined the anomalies discovered during the pressure tests and concluded they did not present a significant cause for concern. However, it's important understand that the actions taken at that precise moment aligned with standard operating procedures. Hindsight always paints a different picture with its perspective," he said.

"Standard operating procedures?" With a tone of incredulity, the senator's voice rose. "Those 'procedures' resulted in the loss of eleven lives and the world's most catastrophic environmental disaster!" The Senator from Michigan paused. "Sir would you say that the Oil Company did not commit any wrongdoing?" he asked.

In spite of the accusing tone, Sterling's expression remained unchanged. "I'm not here to question the existence of mistakes. With that being said, it's essential to acknowledge that this was a complicated

operation that involved a number of different parties. The cementing was done by one company, and the rig was operated by TransSea. Our corporation did the only thing it could do... it relied on the expertise of both companies to bring these tasks to a successful conclusion."

Marshall sensed a shift in the room, characterized by collective bracing as the blame began to shift. It was a strategy that was well known: pointing the finger at someone else and spreading the responsibility so thin that it became difficult to identify any single party. Text book. Because of the numerous layers of bureaucracy and the legal maneuvering that everyone in this place appeared to be so skilled at, the truth was becoming increasingly obscured. Just the way some planned it.

The lawyer from TransSea, who had harsh features and a voice that sounded like gravel, made the most of the opportunity. "Senator, I want to highlight that The Oil Company directly oversaw the rig's operations and directly participated in the decisions regarding the pressure tests and the integrity of the well. Our client adhered to the protocols established by them as they had leased the platform," he said.

The next person to speak was the attorney from the operator responsible for the cement and sealing the well. Her tone was silky and almost oily. "It's also important to remember that the Oil Company's requirements guided the cementing process and they were there at every step," she said. "If there were issues with the well's integrity or the procedures, the rig operator should have addressed them before the cementing process began."

At this point, the room had become a nothing more than a PR battleground, with both sides meticulously crafting their arguments in an effort to distance themselves from the catastrophe and each other. Marshall's anger simmered beneath the surface as he listened to the back-and-forth, his jaw tight and his fists clenched. They were playing a game, and it made him feel sick to his stomach. Then again that might just be the ulcer he had developed over the past year since the accident.

Now a different voice succeeded in cutting through the din: that of a senator with a Southern drawl and a reputation for being able to cut through the bullshit. Leaning forward, he aimed at Sterling.

"It seems to me, Mr. Sterling, that everyone in this room is responsible for some aspect of this mess.

The 11 men who died in the deepwater oil rig explosion and sinking in the Gulf of Mexico in April 2010 were:

•Jason Anderson: Midfield, Tx
•Bubba Burkeen: Philadelphia, Miss.
•Donald Clark: Newellton, Louisiana
•Stephen Curtis: Georgetown, Louisiana
•Gordon Jones: Baton Rouge, Louisiana
•Roy Kemp: Jonesville, Louisiana
•Karl Kleppinger: Natchez, Miss.
•Keith Manuel: Gonzales, Louisiana
•Dewey Revette: State Line, Mississippi
•Shane Roshto: Liberty, Mississippi
•Adam Weise: Yorktown, Texas

No bodies were recovered from the rig.

Rest In Peace

The American people want to know: who will take responsibility? Who will begin the process of recovery? And of course who will pay?" he asked.

"Yes, this matter is our responsibility, and we will make it right, but what's the best way to do that?" asked Sterling sincerely.

The question lingered in the air, permeating a weight of anticipation. Marshall felt a surge of hope, a fleeting belief that someone might break through the corporate doublespeak and express what was needed. This was a fleeting belief. The expression on Sterling's face remained one of professionalism.

"Senator, our company remains committed to minimizing the loss of life and property resulting from this spill. We have already set aside many billions of dollars to clean up the spill and compensate those affected. I have stated that this was not just a failure of our system; rather, it was a failure of multiple systems," he said. It was the oldest dance in politics and corporate business… the reverse game. It was a textbook example of blaming others for what you are most guilty of. A classic.

The realization that nothing was going to change gradually replaced Marshall's hopes, which had been dwindling for some time. The oil kept pouring into the Gulf of Mexico, suffocating everything it came into contact with but while each company attempted to shift the blame as much as possible workers were out there trying to seal the well.

There was more testimony, more accusations, and more denials during the hearing, which dragged on for six and a half hours. Despite exerting significant pressure to obtain answers, the Senators encountered the same carefully crafted responses and polished defenses. By the end of the day, neither resolution nor improvement had occurred.

Marshall continued to linger, his mind racing with anger and frustration as the room began to empty out. This should have been about responsibility and justice for the men who lost their lives not to mention justice for the communities that the spill had initially devastated. On the other hand, it had become a show, a media circus in which the truth was concealed beneath layers of legal jargon and spin from the corporations.

Marshall went outside and discovered Mercer sitting by himself with his head in his hands. Mercer did not utter a single word. Marshall simply sat down next to him, his presence providing a sense of calm and solace amidst the turmoil. Although he blamed him in part for what had happened he did have compassion and understanding of what Mercer was going through… arrogant bastard that he was.

"This is something that they are never going to admit, is it?" Mercer inquired.

Marshall spoke, his voice hollow, "No," he responded in a hushed tone. "No, they're not."

The burden of everything going on was significant, and they sat in silence for a while. Despite the fact that the proceedings may have been over both men knew that the response was far from over.

The tone of Marshall's voice was low and soft, "They'll continue to fight over the blame. And while they're doing that, the oil continues to spill, and the damage continues to disperse. And nobody is going to pay for it—at least not in most cases," he said with sadness in his voice.

Mercer reached over and gently squeezed his hand. "Let's us do it. We need to and I can make them pay for it in ways that even they are not even capable of comprehending," he said. Mercer had converted.

Marshall gave a slight nod while his eyes continued to watch folks leaving the hearing. He was aware that Mercer was correct. There was a significant distance between this sterile hearing rooms in Washington DC and the Gulf of Mexico. However, folks in Power and the American public were coming to grips with the repercussions of what had and was occurring in the Gulf. Most now understood that it would continue to impact their lives for many years to come. The real work of healing, rebuilding, and making things right would remain on hold, a distant hope amidst a sea of uncertainty and money, as the blame-assignment game persisted.

While they were sitting there, watching the last of the light leave, Marshall made a solemn promise to himself in silence. Despite the possibility of not finding justice now or in the upcoming hearings, Marshall was determined not to silence the truth. He would remember and fight, in his own way, to make sure that the real story—the story of what was lost and who was ultimately responsible—would not be forgotten. They might pass the blame around, but he would remember and tell the truth to anyone that would listen for all long as it would take.

When it was all done the congressional committee investigating the "accident" issued its final report about TransSea as well as The Oil Corporation. It said that the most prominent and consistent feature of the company's organizational culture is that it is one of discipline, blame and zero tolerance for mistakes. It said that the company gave "little consideration" to workers' on-rig behavior which could pose serious safety hazards, like fatigue, distraction, communication failures, or defective equipment due to poor maintenance, according to the semi confidential report.

Some of the criticisms of TransSea came directly from its oil rig workers and include a lack of communication from Management and a total unwillingness to hear out or address employee concerns. 9 of the 11 workers killed on the Deepwater Sky were TransSea employees. The company, which owns the biggest fleet of offshore oil platforms in the world, maintains 15 rigs in Europe's North Sea, along with 12 in the Gulf.

For the report, congressional investigators had experts in offshore oil drilling visit four TransSea rigs and interview about 100 workers and managers. The report indicated that on more than one rig workers told them that managers conducted "bullying, aggression, harassment, humiliation and intimidation" on workers deemed "not on the team". The report said workers were demoralized, had little respect for their supervisors, and were stressed — a factor which did and could cause "potential safety implications."

The Gulf disaster gave the report huge importance. For months, The Oil Corporation had attempted to pin the blame for the disaster on the TransSea rig itself. In U.S. Senate hearings, Oil Corporation officials agreed with that argument, saying that "offshore oil and gas production projects begin and end with the operator. While TransSea senior officials stayed on dry land, venturing offshore only on "VIP trips with superficial tours," The Oil Corporation said TransSea allowed the Deepwater Sky to fall into disrepair, says the report. And even offshore, Transocean had few safety representatives on its rigs, and those which were offshore "met infrequently." Others have called both TransSea and The Oil Corporation "the worst offenders" in instilling safe workplace procedures for drilling.

CHAPTER 10

A Public Outcry
'Honey, Let's Drive the new Hummer to the Protest!'

Only a few locals stood on the courthouse steps at the start of the demonstration, holding signs with hastily scrawled slogans. The faces of the individuals were weathered and frustrated when Marshall saw them on the evening news. They were a diverse group of people, including fishermen, environmentalists, and residents who had spent their entire lives along the Gulf Coast. The footage showed them chanting, their voices rising above the din of traffic; however, it was evident that they were just the beginning, the first tremor of something much larger. It wasn't until the following week that the tremor turned into an earthquake.

As Marshall was standing on the edge of the crowd, he could feel the ground beneath him vibrating with the energy of the hundreds of people who were there. Within 30 minutes the crowd grew to included more than 1000! They came from all over the southland; New Orleans, Biloxi, Mobile, Pensacola and carrying banners that appeared to be battle flags flailing in the breeze. The air was thick with the smell of sweat, sunscreen, and the ever-present tang of crude oil. The overall atmosphere was also thick with humidity at a temperature well above 90 degrees. Even here, about a 50 mile distance from the Gulf, the odor lingered, serving as a constant reminder of the catastrophe that they had all gathered to raise their voices against.

Even though the Gulf itself was a battleground of clean up, the fighting had now moved to the streets. The issue now extended far beyond the oil spilling into the ocean. It grew to encompass the destruction of livelihoods and ecosystems, the breach of trust and the lack of corporate responsibility and transparency. The people, particularly those who had suffered the greatest losses, were making their voices heard. The natives had become restless.

A local artist hastily painted a mural as the backdrop, transforming the local park into a makeshift protest stage. The mural showed a pelican struggling to lift its oil-covered wings. The image was gloomy and impactful, and it served to further exacerbate the already tense environment. Marshall was able to sense the anger, frustration, and desperation expressed in every shouted slogan and raised fist of rebelliousness. As he made his way closer and weaved through the dense crowd the anger was easily observable. Folks were pissed. Businesses were closing left and right and real answers were few and far between.

In an amazing turn around Mercer had now become an advocate for the clean up and Marshall and others took notice as did Corporate management. Because of his transformation he was made known that his days at the company were numbered. Bu the disaster

Spontaneous Demonstrations sprang up not just across the Gulf and USA but around the world!

had changed him profoundly and Marshall could tell he was different. He already arrived and was standing close to the front of the room, his gaze fixed on the person who was speaking at the podium when Marshall showed up. Mercer had been attending these demonstrations since the beginning, and his enthusiasm for the cause had grown with each new report of damage and each new revelation of corporate negligence. Marshall admired him for it, despite the fact that he was not always able to match his level of zeal. He was furious; that much was true, but Mercer was now on fire with a passion to get this fixed and not let it happen ever again. And if it cost him his job? So be it.

Today's speaker was an older man. His voice had become rougher over the years as a result of exposure to salt air and cigarette smoke. He was a fisherman, one of the many individuals whose means of subsistence had abruptly disappeared. The speaker's words were unfiltered and unpolished, but they struck a chord deep within the hearts of the people in the crowd listening.

"They tell us it'll get better," the man yelled into the microphone, his voice breaking with the intensity of his feelings. "Some claim they'll clean up the oil, bring back the fish, and restore our lives to back to the way they were. Bullshit! I've lived and fished these waters all my life and they are completely wrong. Not only do they not know what they don't know, but they also don't care! They remain securely ensconced in their boardrooms, counting their profits, while we drown in the mess they made," he said. "Enough, enough, enough!"

Marshall 's heart rate quickened as a result of the wave of sound that washed over him as the crowd roared in agreement. However, despite their harshness, the man's words were accurate. Despite the fact that the oil companies and the government had all made promises, the reality was quite different. The beaches from Florida to Texas continued to be assaulted, the marshes continued to deteriorate, and the fish and birds, once abundant, became increasingly scarce as each day passed.

A young woman with dark eyes and a determined demeanor took the stage along with another speaker. His voice was such that it cut through the background noise like a knife. It was Mercer! Someone who was actually there and had spent years working in the oil business. AS he stepped to the mic to perhaps end his career (the corporation did not allow its employees to make public statements or speak with the media and every employee had to sign a non-disclosure agreement to keep the company's secrets.) the passion Mercer exuded in his voice was new and extremely noticeable. Marshall. Although skeptical at first, came to appreciate the new Mercer.

During his talk, Mercer cried out, his voice rising in pitch. "Please people understand. This isn't just about the oil!" he said. "Their's is a system that places a higher value on profit than on people or the planet. A system that places a higher priority on short-term gains rather than on health! Rather than being a symptom of a much larger disease, this spill is a symptom of a disease that we can no longer ignore. If we fail to implement any changes or hold these businesses accountable, this issue will happen again and again, and the consequences will be even more severe," he said. The crowd roared approval.

Marshall was able to observe the crowd's response, which consisted of a dull roar that gradually transformed into a focused intensity. He also noticed two men in suits taking pictures and video. They were either corporate security men or the FBI. More signs and banners were showing up. These signs were more than just pieces of cardboard; they were declarations of war. They were held by the individuals most affected by the spill. They were going to insure that the companies responsible were to be held accountable for this catastrophe. And the protestors made it quite clear that they were also against the politicians who had made it all possible.

Moreover they were against a system that had let them down protecting the fragile Gulf waters.

Someone in the crowd yelled out, "Boycott the Oil Companies!" and the chant quickly spread throughout the crowd so that others could join in. 'Boycott Oil! 'Boycott Oil! 'Boycott Oil!' It wasn't long before the cry reverberated throughout the entire park, and the sound reverberated throughout the city like thunder.

"Put a stop to Oil! Put a stop to Drilling!" the crowd then chanted. While unrealistic it did help to vent the community's frustration.

Marshall also started shouting, the words bursting out of his chest with a force that took him by surprise. After what seemed like forever he finally experienced a sense of purpose and a real connection to the local people. They were all in this together because they had experienced the same loss and shared the same level of outrage. Following the demonstration, the crowd began to march, and as they moved through the streets, their numbers continued to grow. The local and state police showed up. Some people participated in the activity, while others simply observed it from their car or home windows. The chants became louder and more insistent as the cars honked in unison to show support. The city, which was normally so lively and interesting, had turned into a stage for expressing their rage and suffering, and their desire for justice.

As they moved along with the crowd of people, Marshall walked next to Mercer with their hands intertwined. Their riff was healed and over. His determination and the fire in his eyes filled Marshall with pride. Gone was the cocky corporate suit! Together they become something bigger than themselves. They were not just fighting for themselves but for the Gulf of Mexico's future, and for the countless lives the spill had disrupted.

But Marshall was unable to shake the nagging doubt that was lurking in the back of his mind as they marched. Is this outcry going to be sufficient? Would the protests and voices they raised make any difference? Would leaders just wait them out, hoping the world would forget and move on? He feared that the answer to all three questions was… yep.

The crowd eventually gathered in front of the regional headquarters of the oil company, which was a sleek building with glass frontage that stood in stark contrast to not only the other building in the area but also the grit and determination of the people who were now outside. It was getting ugly. The demonstrators pushed forward, raising their signs to a louder level and echoing their chants off the walls. A line of law enforcement officers stood between them and the building, encircling them. Their faces were expressionless, and their hands were supported by batons. Many of the police had relatives who worked on the rigs or in the refineries.

"Oil company oil company… we see you, we see

you!" they yelled over and over. "We see, we see… the greedy side of you!"

The chant, a battering ram of sound, was rhythmic and relentless, directed against the carefully constructed veneer of the corporation. Marshall was aware of the tension that was present in the crowd— a feeling of an imminent confrontation that caused concern. He had no idea what would happen after that, but he was aware that the crowd would not stop or slow down, not now.

Mercer abruptly separated herself from him and pushed his way through the crowd. Despite Marshall's attempts to get him to stop, Mercer continued to keep his view fixed on the structure in front of him. As he followed him, Marshall experienced a surge of both admiration and fear. The situation caused his chest to heave as Mercer made his way to the front of the crowd and was standing no more than a few feet away from the police line. Mercer displayed his sign in a prominent manner, which Marshall had not seen before. In spite of its simplicity, which consisted of only a few words written in thick black marker, it was able to get to the core of everything… on one side it said;

"These lives are not disposable!" And the other side said; "Fuc the Oil Corporation!" It was heartfelt if not eloquent and it would coast Mercer his job if seen by company management.

Everything seemed to calm down for a brief period

of time, including the chanting, the movement, and even the air itself. Marshall observed Mercer as he remained steadfast at the front, his sign trembling slightly in his grasp and his face displaying a look of defiance. He was spoiling for a fight and the crying man on the rescue boat was long gone. Then, suddenly as if in response to their challenge a window opened on the oil company headquarters and a white sheet was hung out of it. The crowd erupted in cheers, their voices swelling into a unified cry of solidarity. These individuals' collective force was unstoppable, and they continued to push forward, pressing against the police line.

As the police began to shout orders in an effort to contain the surge, Marshall made his way through the crowd to reach Mercer. Too late; the people had found their power and wouldn't compromise! Marshall realized that this was more than just a demonstration it was an unavoidable call for change. It was a reckoning for the Oil Corporation, TransSea

and all the companies in the Gulf. Marshall experienced a feeling that he had not experienced in a very long time: hope. Confronting the corporate monolith that had caused them so much suffering was cathartic. But there was real fear, on both sides that violence might occur. If they could, both Mercer and Marshall believed, the crowd would break thru the police barricades and into the building and just might burn it to the ground. They were that angry.

But even if they lost this war today or tomorrow, they now understood that they were no longer alone. The general public's outcry had now developed into a movement, a force that would continue to grow, push, and demand environmental justice for all. Marshall gave Mercer a gentle pat on the back just as the sun was beginning to set.

"You done gone good!" He said in his cajun accent. A fierce and determined smile appeared on Mercer's face as turned to embrace Marshall. They had become friends, the 'odd couple' of the Gulf Oil industry! They decided to stick together no matter what the future held.

"Don't worry we can help each other with our resumes!" joked Marshall. They both laughed. It was the first lighthearted moment in weeks.

Chapter 11

The Verdict
The Oil Corporation Buys its Way Out

An atmosphere of complete silence pervaded the Federal courtroom. It appeared as though the high vaulted ceilings were amplifying the tense stillness in the air. There were rows of polished wooden benches filled with spectators, journalists, and family members, and the expressions on their faces were a mixture of anticipation and anxiety. With its imposing presence, the judge's bench stood at the forefront of the room, serving as a solemn reminder of the seriousness of the proceedings. It had been more than a year since that fateful night and less than that since the well was capped and the cleanup was still ongoing and would be for a long time.

While waiting for the verdict, Marshall sat among the crowd with his eyes fixed on the front rows. The previous few months had been a whirlwind of demonstrations, hearings, and unending coverage from the media. Anger and frustration had filled the air, but now, as the moment of reckoning drew near, a new tension—a palpable sense of hope mixed with dread—charged the atmosphere. This was a moment of reckoning. Would someone be held accountable?

Ever since Marshall and Mercer had entered the courtroom, Mercer had not let go of the wooden bench, and his knuckles had turned white against the

dark wood of the seat. Mercer wore a fearful and determined expression, his eyes riveted to the target before him. Their efforts, protests, and demands for justice culminated here. Everything had now come to this point and anticipation was strong in the air.

Suddenly, the doors to the courtroom opened, and the members of the jury entered the room. They took their seats with expressions that were carefully neutral. Mercer was a middle-aged man with a composed demeanor, and he watched the juror who held the verdict in his hand to see ion he could sense what the decision might be. Not a chance. Marshall felt his heart pound as he watched, the small piece of paper with the verdict was carrying the weight of an entire nation's hopes and fears.

With a stern face and silver hair, the judge cleared his throat and tapped his gavel. "Order please, order in the court!" he said. A deeper silence descended upon the room, the kind that presses against the eardrums and makes each second feel like it has been going on for an incredibly long time.

"Could you kindly ask the foreperson to move up?" The judge spoke in a tone that reverberated off the walls of the room.

As Mercer sat there, the foreperson held up the envelope that contained the verdict, and his face was completely incomprehensible. The judge gave his a nod, indicating that he should proceed.

The foreperson began by saying, "Ladies and gentlemen of the jury," maintaining a steady tone as he spoke. "We find the defendants— The Oil Corporation, TransSea Inc., and the Acme Cementing Co,—guilty of gross negligence leading

to the Deepwater Sky disaster." A murmured cheer filled the courtroom, a wave of sound that tended to amplify and then diminish as the audience took in the historic words.

"Order, order!" The Judge said banging the gavel.

Marshall experienced a wave of shock and relief at the same time as did most of the audience. They were victorious, but it was a victory that was bittersweet. The Gulf of Mexico was still grappling with the aftermath of the oil spill and the actual harm had already occurred. Meanwhile Oil Corporation had more money than God so any monitory penalty would essentially just be a slap on the wrist. But it was a good first step.

Despite this, the foreperson went on, "We also find that the various parties involved share the responsibility for the disaster, Because the degree of negligence varies, the court will be in charge of determining the appropriate penalties and compensation," the jury Forman concluded.

The words hovered in the air, a constant reminder that despite the establishment of the victim's guilt, the fight for justice remained and would for some time. Mercer's eyes were wet with tears that Marshall had not yet shed. Mercer had exerted significant effort and sacrifice to reach this juncture. When he told his wife what he planned to do she packed a suitcase, left and filed for divorce. And where the company got wind of his off hours activities he was immediately and unceremoniously fired. Now, with the verdict firmly in place, it was evident to him that the journey was just starting. The judge took control of the courtroom, his voice carrying a sense of authority.

"We're going to move on to the sentencing phase at this point," the Judge said. "In one week, the court will meet again to determine the necessary fines and compensatory measures," the gavel was lowered. "This Court is now in recess!"

Immediately after that,, and the courtroom was instantly filled with a flurry of joy. Reporters were frantically searching for interviews, lawyers were gathering their papers, and spectators were hugging each other, their emotions raw and although conflicted still joyous. Taking in the magnitude of what had just occurred, Marshall and Mercer sat in stunned silence with these weird smiles. Mercer talked first, "I, I just can't believe it," he said. His voice was shaking. "So in reality, they are responsible, right?"

With his thoughts racing, Marshall nodded his head. "It's a step in the right direction. It is, however, merely a step. We have a very long way to go after this! And I fear they will find a way to weasel out on payin a dime!" he said.

They exited the courtroom together and passed through the hallway crowd where they saw several members of senior management from other The Oil

Corporation and TransSea... perhaps more importantly the company officials saw then and it was obvious they were not please. The courtroom lobby was now a swarm of press people, with cameras flashing and microphones thrusting toward anyone they could possibly capture. Marshall could hear snippets of interviews, as well as the excitement and disbelief in the voices of the reporters speaking.

"Finally, justice has prevailed!"

"This decision is a watershed moment!"

While leaving the building, Marshall and Mercer temporarily disconnected from the chaos. Before the storm of media and public opinion engulfed them once more, they were standing in the cool, quiet of the courthouse steps, touching their shoulders and sharing a moment of calm before the storm engulfed them once more.

With a solemn expression on his face, Marshall turned to face Mercer. "I guarantee you be a surprise!" he said. What are the next steps?"

Mercer inhaled deeply and maintained his gaze. "We're now gonna work to enforce those penalties. We not only want them to guarantee equitable compensation but we want them also to ensure adequate funding for the cleanup efforts and hold the companies accountable for their neglectful actions," he asserted. Marshall nodded, his determination now becoming more resolute.

"In addition, we'll continue to advocate for the changes to make sure this never happens ever again," Mercer said, "I've never been so ashamed too be an Oil man in all my life!"

Upon reflection they both felt that the verdict was a true victory, but it also reminded them of the ongoing struggle that would take year. The Gulf remained scarred, the impacted lives continued to suffer, and the quest for justice remained unresolved.

As they made their way away from the courthouse, Marshall cast a glance back at the structure. The din of the celebrating crowd grew louder, encircling the building. In the past, the courthouse had served as a battlefield, but today, a certain degree of justice had been accomplished. The days and months ahead

would reveal the true test, which would be the implementation of the verdict, the realignment of priorities, and the healing of a wounded region.

The first week following the verdict was a whirlwind of activity. The media coverage of the case was unrelenting, with news reports and talk shows dissecting every facet of the case, the verdict, and the implications for the oil industry's future. Because their faces became recognizable to viewers all over the country, Marshall and Mercer found themselves in the spotlight more frequently than they liked or had actually anticipated. Over the course of time, they participated in interviews, press conferences, and meetings with lawyers and activists. Although exhausted, they kept going because they knew their fight was not over.

When the day of sentencing arrived, the courtroom was once again filled to capacity with spectators, and the atmosphere was saturated with anticipation. While waiting for the proceedings to begin, Marshall and Mercer took their seats, with nervous anticipation. An almost overwhelming sense of finality pervaded the audience. The previous week had been a blur of both anticipation and anxiety. The proceedings Today would finally reveal the consequences of the verdict.

When the judge entered the courtroom, there was a momentary pause in the proceedings. The legal teams of the three defendants were present, and their expressions remained as unmoved as they had been throughout the proceedings. Not one member of the management teams of the three company's were in attendance. The grizzled attorney leading the prosecution seemed determined. The defense teams were tense, and by their facial expressions you could tell that the stakes were extremely high.

"Please rise!" Said the court bailiff. The judge intoned, "This court of the 5th District will come to order!" As a result everyone in the room stood as one and held their breath. "Please be seated."

The Judge began "The court has considered the presented evidence and all the arguments and the court is prepared to render its judgment. The penalties in light of the jury's findings, which determined that the defendant had engaged in gross negligence, are significant," he said.

The tone of the judge's voice was authoritative, and there was a sense of solemnity that emphasized the degree of seriousness of the decision. Starting with the oil company, he detailed the fines and compensation amounts imposed during the sentencing investigation. He decreed the staggering numbers to account for both the immediate cleanup costs, the long-term environmental damage and the economic hardships faced by local businesses. Despite being a previously unheard-of figure, most felt it fell far short of covering the necessary ground for true reparations.

The Judge announced that the oil company would have to pay a total of twenty billion dollars in fines and compensation. The audience responded to the announcement with a mixture of approval and apprehension. However, for those directly affected, it was both a victory and a small step towards what was truly needed. Although it was a significant and marked a milestone more would be needed.

The next companies to face their own set of fines and compensation demands were the Cementing company and TransSea the rig owner. Despite a slight reduction in severity, the sentences remained significant due to their roles in the disaster. The announcement of each final figure filled the courtroom with a tableau of mixed emotions. Each figure not only signified a step towards addressing the enormous damage, but also acted as a reminder of the ongoing work. The plaintiff was less than pleased already talking about appealing the decision.

Marshall felt a multitude of conflicting emotions as the Judge brought down his gavel for the final time, signaling the end of these proceedings. There would be others and it was clear that their fight was far from over, despite the fact that the verdict had been a monumental achievement. But the corporate

hesitancy in its implementation showed they would fight it and it's a long way from being resolved.

Following their departure from the courthouse, Marshall and Mercer wore expressions that conveyed happiness, relief and exhaustion. Despite their victory it was abundantly clear that their fight to make it right was not yet over. They needed to ensure the implementation of the penalties, distribute the compensation to those in need, and make significant adjustments to drilling procedures prevent future catastrophes.

Marshall turned to look at Mercer as they made their way through the city, leaving the media frenzy in the rearview mirror. Mercer's face was etched with a smile for he first time since that night. Despite the fact that they'd achieved a significant victory, the Coast was still struggling, and the injuries it caused were still visible. The cleanup process, providing assistance to the communities, and ensuring the lessons learned from this disaster led to genuine and long-lasting change, were essential.

They arrived at the park where they had the demonstrations a peaceful place for contemplation. The mural that depicted the pelican that was drenched in oil was still standing, serving as a powerful reminder of what had been lost. Marshall and Mercer sat on a park bench, their hands clasped together, sharing a moment of silence.

The tone of Marshall's voice was low but determined as he stated, "It's not over by a long shot. We must remain vigilant in our fight for justice because you know those suits gonna fight this at every step. It's their nature to resist change that's why we are here," he said.

Mercer nodded, his eyes reflecting the sunset. "Since we've already made this far, we're not gonna to stop now. There's a need for us to be here. We must make certain we're not merely a headline but rather a real turning point!" he said. "Maybe we should start a company together to help advise community groups about the settlement. Besides I'm gonna need a new job!" They both laughed,

Chapter 12

The Real Cost of Oil
We are Addicted

The Gulf Coast, which had been a place of lush vegetation, fertile waters and vibrant southern culture in the past, now bore the burden of an unapproachable reality. The landscape, adorned with the rusting hulks of abandoned fishing boats and the skeletal remains of trees blackened by crude oil, served as a stark reminder of the price one must pay for progress and America's thirst for cheap gasoline. Despite some cleaning of the beaches, the oily sheen remained in some areas, a cruel testament to the spill's aftermath. Folks reported tar balls on the beaches as long as five years after the spill.

The two individuals who were front and center that day, Marshall and Mercer, had made their way back to the coast in order to observe the aftermath of the disaster and the ongoing efforts to recover from it. The sun was harsh, casting an unrelenting glare off the water as it seemed to mock the idea of recovery. Together the two men, who had become unlikely friends, had been traveling through the Gulf coast from Texas to Florida, meeting with locals, and observing the prolonged and excruciating process of environmental restoration.

On the outskirts of a devastated town, Tom Lennon, a local fisherman, sat with Marshall and Mercer in a small office. The office was a claustrophobic and disorganized place, with maps affixed to the walls and stacks of paperwork and books that were all over the floor. Recounting the personal cost of the spill Tom, a burly man with sun-weathered skin and eyes that spoke of a long battle with the sea, described the spill's impact on his life.

"I've been fishing these waters since I was a kid," Tom said, his voice as rough as gravel from his years. "My father taught me, and his father guided me. My blood is full of it. However, at this moment —Now? I've got nothing," he said, pausing for a moment and gazing out the window at the empty docks. With no fish I have no way to earn a living. It also doesn't help if the Gulf Water eats the hull of your $200k fiberglass boat!"

The subsequent silence was difficult to bear because it was replete with unspoken loss. An expression of compassion could be seen in Mercer's eyes as he extended his hand to touch Tom. "We wanna help in any way that we can," he said. "However, the sad thing is the process is slow and the damage significant, greater than we could have anticipated."

With a stoic expression on his face, Tom nodded his head in agreement. "Dad's true and you have my gratitude for sure. I see the same things every day: families struggling to make ends meet and boats that are unable to move let alone fish. Despite the removal of oil from the beaches, its presence persists in the water and the damn dispersant they're using is

worse than the oil!" he said.

The faded photographs of bustling fishing fleets and family pictures with 3 foot fishes were one of the things that Marshall looked at as he walked around the room. There was a striking disparity between those happier times and the present-day. "Like you I have lived these waters all my life. It may never be the same and the recuperation process is going to take some time," Marshall offered. "The money from the verdict might be helpful if used appropriately, but we must and we are going to insure its distribution and the money gets to the right places... businesses like yours."

Tom's look was intense, and his voice spoke with a sense of determination. "I really do hope so. However, we can't simply measure the cost in dollars and cents. The simultaneous eradication of culture, customs, and the loss of way of life is being lost... that is the true cost!" the aging fisherman said. "I hope they get that."

The scene was sobering, both inside the small office and outside on the empty docks. The magnitude of the damage was sometimes, in fact often times, unnoticed and certainly under appreciated. The damage and media coverage frequently overshadowed the tireless efforts of the recovery crews. Later that day as Marshall and Mercer strolled along the beach, workers wearing heavy protective gear continued the laborious task of cleaning up the beach one scoop at a time. As the clean up crew slowly combed through the sand, their sight served as a reminder of the enormous scope of the problem.

As they walked, Mercer's phone rang with a notification about the latest news. He took a quick glance at it, and as Mercer read the headline, his face became more tense. "The office of Senator Johnson has just issued a statement," Mercer said as he showed Marshall the screen showing the statement. "They propose reducing the funding for environmental restoration by 30%! They argue that the expense is excessive and suggest redirecting the funds to other components," Mercer read.

Anger began to rise in Marshall. "I'm not surprised! But how are they able to do that? The Gulf of Mexico hasn't recovered by a long shot," he said. "Families are still experiencing hardships, and the ecosystems are still recovering. The issue is people's lives and livelihoods, not just money. Dem cats tis about the money, eh?" his eyes filled with gloom.

"We were aware that this might occur," said Mercer. "I trust these assholes about as far as I can throw them! The struggle to secure funding is not yet over. On the contrary, it's going to become even more difficult and they're gonna fight us at every turn!"

On their way down the road, they contemplated the harsh reality of their situation. The Gulf Coast was embroiled in a conflict between political pressures that sought to undermine the recovery process and the struggle of recovery. Despite winning the legal battle, the actual work of paying for the rebuilding was far from settled. It would take years if ever.

In the evening, they sat on the porch of a Bed and Breakfast in the neighborhood. The peaceful beauty of the sunset appeared to be in stark contrast to the agony and struggle that they had witnessed throughout the day. While Marshall was looking out over the water, he noticed that the waves were calm now, but that they still carried the remnants of their turbulent past. Sometimes the wave action would create off looking brownish bubbles.

"Do ya believe we ever return to the place we were?" In his cajun accent Marshall asked the question in a tone that mixed optimism and anxiety. Mercer inhaled deeply and maintained his view as Marshall did so. "I have faith that we will, but it's going to require a tremendous deal of effort. But it's like Oil baron John D Rockefeller said in 1903 "Don't be afraid to give up the good to go for the great!" Mercer said for he was a learned man with an Ivy League education. "We mustn't let up, nor allow this fight to die down. The public has a short memory and there's too much at stake," he said.

Feeling the weight of his words, Marshall nodded. "Not only did we measure the price of oil in monetary figures, but also in the disrupted lives and the ruined natural world it caused," Mercer continued. "The spill brought to light the precarious nature of the Gulf environment, as well as the precariousness of the communities that were dependent on it. We know but Washington and Europe don't," he said.

When they were walking back to their B & B room, the stars were just beginning to appear in the night sky, which was completely clear. The beauty of the night, seemingly promising renewal, revealed light even in the midst of the darkest days. Late into the night, Marshall and Mercer engaged in a conversation that was a mixture of introspection and talk of the future. They talked about the challenges ahead, the importance of distributing the funding to the communities, and the need to maintain the momentum of their advocacy. They also talked about who was gonna pay their expenses.

"Our fight for justice is not yet over!" Marshall said with determination in his voice, We're just gettin' started. It's imperative that we maintain vigilance and continue to advocate for the changes that will bring about a genuine difference," Mercer said with

a determination in his eyes nodding his head. "Let us do it! At this point, we can't return to our previous ways so there's no way but forward. The Gulf of Mexico needs our help and we must make certain that the lessons we've learned from this will result in genuine and long-lasting operational and regulatory change... and we need to make sure that The Oil Corporation pays every single damn bill!"

It appeared as though the Gulf Coast, visible from their window, was breathing with cautious optimism as they both drifted off to sleep. Although recovery was difficult, the determination of those who fought for justice guided those seeking help. Despite the high oil price, there was an unwavering dedication to rebuilding and restoring the lost.

Marshall's heart was heavy but hopeful as he looked out over the coast the following morning, as they were getting ready to leave. The Gulf Coast was a place of resiliency and strength. Folks who live there have spunk and despite the fact that the wounds caused by the disaster were severe, the spirit of the people continues to be unbroken. The journey that lay ahead was one that they would face together, driven by a shared commitment to make things right. The fight for justice, recovery funds, and the region's future was not even close to being over.

The sun was rising behind Marshall and Mercer as they drove down the coast, with all the closed businesses reminding them that their work was far from finished. Despite the lengthy nature of the Gulf Coast fight, every ounce of effort put forth would prove to be well worth it. Despite the fact that the price of drilling for oil had been high now the price of inaction was significantly higher. They continued resolute in their desire to witness the Gulf Coast they both loved recover and flourish once more.

Well MC-252: Capped July 15, 2010

U.S. Coastal Waters Affected by the Gulf Oil Spill

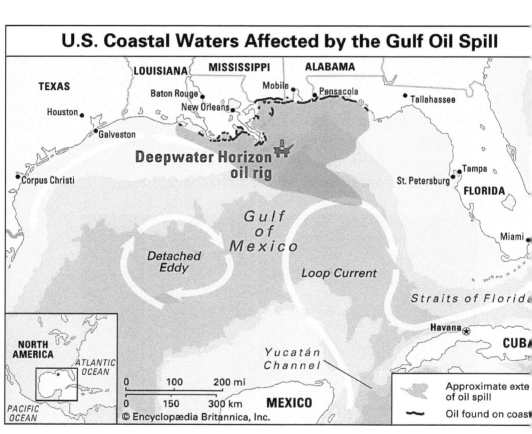

TEXAS

LOUISIANA MISSISSIPPI ALABAMA

Mobile Pensacola
Baton Rouge
New Orleans Tallahassee
Houston
Galveston

Deepwater Horizon
oil rig

Corpus Christi St. Petersburg Tampa

FLORIDA

Gulf
of
Mexico

Miami

Detached
Eddy Loop Current

Straits of Florida

Havana CUBA

NORTH
AMERICA ATLANTIC
OCEAN

Yucatán
Channel

PACIFIC
OCEAN

| 0 | 100 | 200 mi |
| 0 | 150 | 300 km |

MEXICO

© Encyclopædia Britannica, Inc.

Approximate extent
of oil spill

Oil found on coast

Chapter 13

The Frog in the Pan
Is Mankind Suicidal?

When the sun rose in the early morning, the Gulf Coast shone brightly, and the shimmering waters reflected the region's revitalized spirit. Communities were flourishing in a revitalized business environment, while greenery was reclaiming its place and vibrant marine life was returning to the reefs. Vibrant colors now flooded the once ruined landscape. Marshall and Mercer had labored tirelessly to bring about this moment, which was a manifestation of the recovery they had worked so hard to achieve.

Their mission was complete but the recovery wasn't. Everywhere you looked, you could see signs of recovery. Oil that had once tainted the beaches seemed gone the cleaning had restored them to their original condition. In the past, the docks where fishermen worked were empty, but now they were bustling with new activity. The vibrant colors of freshly painted boats and the aroma of the sea air served as a testament to the hard-won victory.

The centerpiece of the celebration was a lively event that celebrated not only the recovery but also the community's unity and determination. The Gulf Festival took place in a small coastal town, serving as the central hub of the celebration. The festival grounds were teeming with enthusiastic fun. The air was filled with the melodies of local musicians and the joyful laughter of children. Colorful banners decorated stalls offering a wide variety of products, from local crafts to food to environmental literature.

Mercer stood near a booth from 'Ocean Future' that aimed to educate guests about the significance of environmental protection of the Gulf. While Mercer was there, he observed families coming in and having animated conversations about the importance of protecting their natural resources and sustainable fishing practices. The sight served as a powerful reminder of the progress that they'd made so far. Mercer faced Marshall, his eyes gleaming with pride. "Look at this! It is so amazing to see how the community has come together to support one another. Very cool!" he said. "They're not simply celebrating; rather, they are actively participating in the process of shaping their future!"

"You're so full of shite!" Marshall said with a laugh. "But yes you're right the transformation is truly remarkable to see. I guess the fight was not just about surviving the catastrophe; rather, it was about all of us developing a fresh perspective on what the future holds. I mean look at us!"

"What do you mean?" Asked Mercer.

"Well that day we were about to come to blows and we's a difference as day and night. Now? I calls you me friend and I trust you! 'Mwen fè ou konfyans' he said in Creole meaning the same thing.

"Mercer you are now an adopted southerner. You may have been a yankee by birth but you now a rebel by choice and I am damn proud of ya!"

The festival was a celebration of more than just recovery; it was a demonstration of the community's ability to persevere and the success of the advocacy efforts they had undertaken. Marshall and Mercer received an enthusiastic round of applause as they approached the stage for their scheduled speeches. The common experience of rebuilding united everyone in the crowd, and their faces displayed a mosaic of different ages, ranging from locals to folks from around the country.

The moment Marshall stepped onto the stage, his heart began to swell with emotion as he looked out at the audience. He resisted the urge to cry.

"This day is more than just a celebration of the recovery process. It's a testament to the things that together we're capable of accomplishing. We refuse to accept defeat, and we will continue to work tirelessly for a better future for the Gulf. The catastrophe that occurred in the Spring of 2010 on the Deepwater Sky was a tragedy, but the silver lining is that it also served as a driving force behind change. We've witnessed the environment's resilience, this community's strength, and collective action's power. Long live the gulf!" Mercer concluded. Now Marshall stepped to the mic and after a moment… "What he said!" And the crowd busted up laughing. He then started to speak in Louisiana creole.

"Gòlf la se lavi nou!
Ansanm nou pral genyen.
Pwoteje lanmè
nou ak lavi nou!"

*"The Gulf is our life!
Together we will win.
Protect our ocean and sea life!"*

They received a powerful affirmation of their journey in the form of the cheers and applause, which followed. Mercer joined Marshall at the podium, his voice steady and full of hope as he spoke. "We fought for accountability, adequate funding, and a future in which a spill of this magnitude, will never happen again. As we celebrate today, we're not only commemorating the restoration of our coastline, but also actualizing our vision for a better world. Our efforts have transformed a gloomy chapter into a ray of light. Long live the Gulf!"

Following the Speech's and the enthusiastic response, the festival continued with performances by local artists from the surrounding area headlined by Jimmy Buffett. The music reflected the rich cultural heritage of the region, featuring everything from dixieland to rock-n-roll. The dancers' joyful abandon embodied a celebration of the revitalized vitality of the Gulf Coast. People from the surrounding area who had survived the storm, both literally and figuratively, attended the festival. In the process of making their way through the crowd, Marshall and Mercer engaged in conversations with locals and listened to the stories they shared. They encountered fishermen who had returned to their boats for the first time in more than a year with a renewed sense of hope, environmentalists who were working to ensure that the region would continue to recover, and families who had come together to rebuild their lives. It was inspiring to both of them.

An elderly woman approached them, her semi-forced smile conveying both despondency and optimism. Years of experience etched her face with wisdom. "I remember the days when the water was thick with oil, the beaches were dark, and the skies seemed to weigh on everyone. Mercer gestured around the festival, pointing to the bustling activity, and said, "Now, it's like a new beginning." We've come a very long way."

As he looked at all this, Marshall's heart was filling. "Your positive attitude and determination have been an essential component in this process of recuperation. This is only possible because of the spirit that you possess," he told a local fisherman.

It was sunset time so Marshall and Mercer discovered a secluded spot that overlooked the water and watched the sun cast a golden glow before slipping into the water. The Gulf of Mexico, once scarred by disaster, now glowed with the promise of a brighter future, proof of what few can do together.

Marshall shifted his attention to Mercer, his tone conveying a sense of contentment as well as that of reflection. "Not only have we accomplished a tremendous deal, this is only the beginning. We need to make sure we put the knowledge we've gained into practice, we need to continue to safeguard this special environment, and never lose sight of the significance of preserving it for future generations. That's the true challenge!"

Mercer nodded his head, "You sound like you are running for office! Yep we have established a solid foundation; however, it's up to each and every one of us to continue to build upon it. Right? We're now in possession of the future that we've fought for, and it's our responsibility to ensure that it lives on and thrives," he said. "It's the least we can do!"

Both Marshall and Mercer took a deep breath as the sun began to set and the stars began to appear. They were filled with a profound sense of accomplishment. Even though the recovery from the oil spill was long and difficult, they came out with a renewed commitment to protecting the Gulf Coast.

During the days that followed, as the two of them

were getting ready to leave they reflected on their journey. They had help to heal the Gulf, revitalized communities, and transforming a disaster into an opportunity for growth and change. They had witnessed all of these things. Despite not having finished their work, their progress served as a powerful example of the impact that advocacy, and collective action by two regular guys can achieve.

Marshall and Mercer knew that their efforts had laid the groundwork for a future in which the lessons of the past had paved the way for a more sustainable and hopeful world with the light of a future without oil showing the way. They both felt privileged to have been a part of that transformation.

With them went the knowledge that their fight had not only helped to heal a region, but that it had also inspired a movement toward a more conscious and compassionate approach to environmental stewardship for the Gulf. Marshall and Mercer carried this knowledge with them during their journey and that knowledge helped to erase the memories of that devastating night or at least make them more manageable. At this point, the future held promise and possibility, but helping the Gulf fully recover would still require significant effort.

"Besides we gots no business drilling dat deep water oil," Marshall concluded. "Might as well be drillin on the damn Moon!"

Enter COREXIT...
The Long-Term Health Effects
of Chemical Dispersants

The use of chemical dispersants, such as COREXIT, during oil spills has always raised significant concerns regarding their long-term health effects. Dispersants are designed to break down oil into smaller droplets, promoting faster degradation and reducing the impact on shorelines. However, their application comes with potential risks to both human health and the environment. Understanding these risks involves examining the specific dispersants, their mechanisms of action, and the potential health impacts observed over time. More than 1,840,000 gallons of oil dispersant was used.

There are Acute Health Effects according to experts. Acute exposure to dispersants, especially for those involved in spill response activities, can lead to immediate health issues. Symptoms reported by spill cleanup workers and responders include:

Respiratory Irritation: Inhalation of dispersant vapors can cause respiratory irritation, manifesting as coughing, wheezing, and shortness of breath. Individuals with pre-existing respiratory conditions may experience exacerbated symptoms.

Dermal Reactions: Direct contact with dispersants can cause skin irritation, rashes, or burns. Some

dispersants contain solvents and surfactants that are known skin irritants.

<u>Systemic Symptoms:</u> Exposure can also lead to systemic symptoms such as headaches, dizziness, nausea, and gastrointestinal issues. These symptoms may be more pronounced if the exposure is prolonged or at high concentrations.

Long-term chronic health effects of dispersants are more challenging to study but are a significant concern due to potential persistent exposure and bioaccumulation. 15 years later research in this area is ongoing but funding is slim.

Some known and suspected effects include:

Respiratory Health: Chronic exposure to chemical dispersants may lead to long-term respiratory issues. Repeated or prolonged exposure to chemical vapors or residues can contribute to chronic bronchitis or asthma. The fine particles from dispersants may also aggravate existing respiratory conditions.

Dermatological Effects: Continued skin exposure can lead to chronic dermatitis or other skin disorders. Persistent irritation or sensitization can cause long-term skin problems, especially among workers who handle these chemicals frequently.

Reproductive & Developmental Risks: Some chemicals in dispersants are suspected of having reproductive and developmental toxicity. For example, certain solvents are known to affect fetal development or fertility, though comprehensive data on dispersants specifically is limited. Animal studies suggest potential risks, but further research is needed to confirm these effects in humans.

Cancer Risk: Components of dispersants, such as benzene, are classified as potential carcinogens. Long-term exposure to these substances could theoretically increase cancer risk, though direct evidence linking dispersants to cancer in humans is still under investigation.

Mental Health Impacts: The psychological effects of exposure to dispersants and involvement in oil spill response activities are also noteworthy. Workers and residents exposed to dispersants may experience stress, anxiety, and depression. The additional stress from dealing with the environmental and economic impacts of the spill can compound these effects. Support for mental health, including counseling and psychological services, is critical in addressing these concerns.

The impact on Marine Life is substantial because dispersants alter the physical and chemical properties of oil and in turn all of which leads to a complex set of negative impacts on marine life:

Fish and Shellfish: Dispersed oil droplets can penetrate deeper into the water column and affect a wide range of marine organisms. Fish and shellfish exposed to these droplets can experience developmental deformities, reduced reproductive success, and increased mortality rates. Studies have shown that exposure can impact the health of fish embryos and larvae, leading to long-term population effects.

Coral Reefs: Coral reefs are highly sensitive to pollution. Dispersants and dispersed oil can damage coral polyps, leading to bleaching, disease, and reduced reproductive rates. The health of coral reefs is crucial for supporting marine biodiversity and protecting coastlines.

There's also overall habitat degradation after it is used. The application of dispersants and the subsequent degradation of oil can have lasting effects on key marine habitats and on humans:

Wetlands & Mangroves: These critical coastal habitats can be adversely affected by both oil and dispersants. Wetlands and mangroves provide essential ecosystem services, such as storm surge protection and wildlife habitat. Damage to these areas can lead to erosion, reduced biodiversity, and loss of ecosystem services.

Seagrass Beds: Seagrass beds are vital for coastal marine life and serve as nursery grounds for many species. Dispersants and oil contamination can inhibit seagrass growth and function, leading to declines in associated marine populations.
Chemical dispersants and the dispersed oil droplets can enter the marine food web, leading to bioaccumulation and biomagnification:

Bioaccumulation: Toxic chemicals in dispersants can accumulate in the tissues of marine organisms over time. This can lead to higher concentrations of toxins in species that are higher up the food chain.

Biomagnification: As these toxins move up the food chain, they become more concentrated. This can have significant effects on apex predators, including marine mammals and birds, as well as on human consumers of seafood.

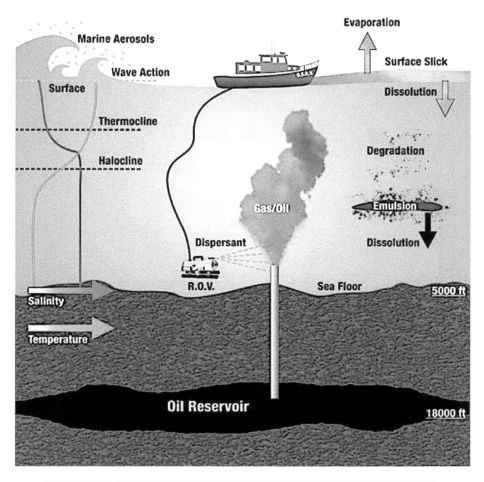

In response to the potential risks associated with dispersants, there has been increased regulation:

Regulatory Frameworks: Agencies like the Environmental Protection Agency (EPA) and the National Oceanic and Atmospheric Administration (NOAA) have established guidelines for the use of dispersants. These guidelines aim to balance the benefits of dispersants in oil spill response with potential risks to human health and the environment.

Testing and Approval: Dispersants undergo rigorous testing before approval for use. However, the effectiveness and safety profiles of different dispersants continue to be evaluated, and new formulations are being developed to reduce toxicity.

Research into the health effects of dispersants is ongoing and includes:

Health Studies: Longitudinal studies are being conducted to track the health outcomes of individuals exposed to dispersants, including workers and residents. These studies aim to identify long-term health effects.

The Environmental Impact Assessments by various government organizations have continued since

2010. Continuous monitoring and research are essential to assess the long-term impacts of dispersants on marine ecosystems. This includes studying the recovery of affected habitats, as well as the effectiveness of restoration efforts.

The long-term health effects of chemical dispersants like COREXIT encompass a range of concerns for both human health and environmental well-being. While dispersants play a critical role in oil spill response, their use comes with potential risks that must be managed carefully. Ongoing research, regulatory oversight, and advancements in dispersant technology are crucial in minimizing these risks and ensuring that future responses to oil spills are both effective and safe. Addressing the health impacts requires a comprehensive approach, including monitoring, prevention, and support for affected individuals and ecosystems.

Follow the Moola!
Can Money Fix the Gulf?

The Deepwater Horizon oil spill, which occurred on April 20, 2010, had profound and far-reaching economic impacts. The disaster not only caused immediate financial losses but also had long-term effects on various sectors. Here's an overview of the key economic impacts from the disaster:

The Fishing Industry
Commercial and Recreational Fishing:
Economic Losses: The oil spill led to significant economic losses for both commercial and recreational fishermen. Immediate fishing closures in affected areas and concerns about contaminated seafood led to decreased revenues. The spill disrupted fishing operations, and many fishermen faced substantial income losses.

Long-Term Effects: Even after the initial response, the fishing industry continued to suffer due to ongoing concerns about seafood safety and the health of fish populations. Many fisheries experienced reduced yields, and recovery was slow. The long-term impact included altered fishing patterns and continued market uncertainties.

Tourism Industry
Reduced Visitor Numbers: The Gulf Coast region, known for its tourism and recreational activities,

experienced a decline in tourism following the spill. The negative perception of oil contamination and concerns about beach cleanliness led to decreased visitor numbers and revenue losses for local businesses.

Economic Recovery Efforts: Tourism-dependent communities faced substantial financial strain. Marketing campaigns and cleanup efforts aimed at restoring the region's reputation were crucial in helping the tourism industry recover. However, the spill's impact on tourism persisted for several years.

Oil & Gas Industry
Operational and Financial Impact:
Increased Costs and Regulation: The spill led to increased operational costs for the oil and gas industry due to heightened safety and environmental regulations. Companies faced regular and more stringent regulatory scrutiny, which resulted in higher compliance costs and changes to drilling procedures and operations.

Liability Compensation:
the oil company and other involved parties faced substantial financial liabilities. The costs associated with cleanup, compensation to affected parties, and legal settlements amounted to billions of dollars. The financial burden also affected investor confidence and industry dynamics.

Legal and Settlement Costs

Legal Costs: The spill resulted in extensive legal battles involving the oil company, Transocean, Halliburton, and other parties. Lawsuits from government agencies, affected businesses, and individuals led to significant legal costs.

Settlement Agreements:

The oil company and other responsible parties entered into settlement agreements totaling billions of dollars. These settlements aimed to compensate affected individuals, businesses, and governmental entities. The payments covered various claims, including economic losses, environmental damage, and health-related expenses.

Environmental & Cleanup Costs

Cleanup Operations: The immediate and extensive cleanup operations were costly. Resources were allocated to contain and recover the oil, mitigate environmental damage, and restore affected areas.

Long-term environmental restoration efforts required significant financial investments. These included projects to rehabilitate ecosystems, restore habitats, and monitor long-term impacts.

Economic Disruption:

Employment and Business Losses: Local businesses, especially those dependent on tourism and fishing, faced economic hardships. Job losses and business closures affected community livelihoods. The spill highlighted the vulnerability of communities dependent on a single industry. Efforts to diversify local economies and build a varied business climate were emphasized in the recovery process.

Insurance Claims:
Insurance Impact: The scale of the disaster led to significant insurance claims, affecting the insurance industry's financial stability. The high costs of claims and settlements influenced insurance practices and coverage terms.

Market Reactions

Investor Confidence: The spill affected investor confidence in the oil and gas industry. The financial repercussions and regulatory changes impacted stock prices and investment decisions in the sector.
The Deepwater Horizon oil spill had wide-ranging and profound economic impacts that extended beyond the immediate aftermath of the disaster.

The fishing and tourism industries faced significant financial losses, while the oil and gas industry dealt with increased costs and regulatory scrutiny. Legal, environmental, and local community impacts further compounded the economic challenges. The disaster highlighted the interconnectedness of economic sectors and underscored the importance of comprehensive response/recovery strategies to address the effects of such catastrophes.

The total financial damage from the Deepwater Horizon oil spill is substantial, involving various costs and financial settlements. Estimates of the total financial impact are often presented in terms of billions of US dollars. Here's a breakdown of the major components:

Cleanup Costs

Immediate Response and Cleanup:
the oil company, along with other parties involved, spent approximately $14 billion on immediate response and cleanup efforts. This includes costs for oil recovery, containment, and mitigation.

Legal Settlements and Fines

Settlement Agreements: the oil company reached several significant settlement agreements. In 2015, the oil company agreed to a settlement of $18.7 billion with the U.S. federal government, five Gulf Coast states, and various local governments. This settlement covered economic and environmental damages as well as penalties. In addition to the settlement, the oil company faced civil and criminal penalties. In 2012, the oil company agreed to pay $4.5 billion in criminal penalties to the government as part of a plea deal.

Compensation Payments:

Claims Payments: the oil company established the Gulf Coast Claims Facility (GCCF) to compensate individuals and businesses affected by the spill. The GCCF paid out approximately $6.3 billion in claims to individuals and businesses affected by the spill.

Environmental Restoration

Restoration Projects: Funding for long-term environmental restoration and monitoring has been significant. The RESTORE Act, which was enacted in 2012, directs 80% of the penalties paid by the oil company to Gulf Coast restoration projects. The total funding for these projects is expected to reach tens of billions of dollars over time, with ongoing investments in ecosystem restoration.

Total Estimated Costs

When combining the costs of cleanup, legal settlements, compensation payments, and environmental restoration, estimates of the total financial damage from the Deepwater Horizon oil spill exceed $60 billion. This figure includes direct costs to the oil company, legal settlements, and the broader economic impact on affected communities.

The total financial damage represents one of the most costly environmental disasters in history, reflecting the extensive and long-lasting impact of the spill on both the environment and the economy.

Deep Drilling!

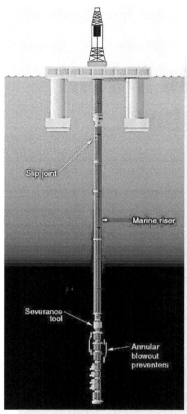

As this is being written in the Fall of 2024, the deepest oil well ever drilled is the Z-44 Chikyu well, located in the Nankai Trough off the coast of Japan. This well, drilled by the Japan Agency for Marine-Earth Science and Technology (JAMSTEC), reached a depth of approximately 23,000 feet below the seafloor back in 2016.

The Z-44 well is part of the Integrated Ocean Drilling Program (IODP) and is notable not just for its depth but also for its scientific significance. It was drilled to study the geological properties and potential seismic hazards in this seismically active region. The Chikyu vessel, equipped with advanced drilling technology, played a crucial role in achieving this record depth. Previously, the record for the deepest oil well was held by the oil company-operated the Deepwater Horizon well in the Gulf of Mexico, which reached a total depth of 20,670 feet before the blowout and the world's worse oil spill in 2010

Workin on the Moon!
By the Numbers...

As of recent estimates, approximately 58,000 to 60,000 people work on oil platforms and related offshore facilities in the Gulf of Mexico. These workers are involved in a wide range of activities, including drilling, production, maintenance, logistics, and support services.

The number of people working on Gulf of Mexico oil platforms can fluctuate depending on the level of activity in the industry, including the number of active drilling rigs, production platforms, and ongoing exploration projects. The workforce is typically composed of a mix of skilled labor, engineers, technicians, and support staff, with many workers employed on a rotational basis, often spending weeks at a time on the platforms before rotating back to shore.

This workforce is essential not only for the operation of the platforms but also for ensuring safety, environmental protection, and efficient production. The oil and gas industry in the Gulf of Mexico is a major employer in the region, contributing significantly to the local and national economy as America searches for oil in the Gulf.

ONLINE INFO SOURCES

https://www.epa.gov/deepwaterhorizon

https://www.restorethegulf.gov/

https://www.nasa.gov/centers-and-facilities/jpl/
nasa-noaa-tech-will-aid-marine-oil-spill-response/

http://www.DCO.USCG.MIL

https://response.restoration.noaa.gov/oil-and-
chemical-spills/oil-spills

https://www.britannica.com/event/Deepwater-
Horizon-oil-spill

https://en.wikipedia.org/wiki
Deepwater_Horizon_oil_spill

http://response.restoration.noaa.gov/
deepwaterhorizon

https://oilspill.fsu.edu/

https://www.mmc.gov/priority-topics/offshore-
energy-development-and-marine-mammals/gulf-of-
mexico-deepwater-horizon-oil-spill-and-marine-
mammals/

<u>Acknowledgments</u>

Deepwater Horizon Hero Doug Brown
National Petroleum Institute
Earth Justice League
Gulf Coast Environmental Association
The State of Louisiana, Media Affairs
The Nature Conservancy
GulfCorps
The Gulf of Mexico Alliance
Restore America's Estuaries
AP Photos Inc.
The Gulf Coast Preservation Society
Ocean Conservancy
Gulf Coast Center for Ecotourism
WildAid Marine
DepositO Photos
Southern Environmental Law Center
The Encyclopedia Britannica
The Natural Resources Defense Council
NOAA
US Dept. of Environmental Protection
US Dept. of the Interior

Books by Author Tom McAuliffe

- **Mr. Mulligan** - *The Life of Champion Armless Golfer Tommy McAuliffe*

- **Nuts!** - *The Life & Times of Gen. Tony McAuliffe*

- **Throttle Up** - *Astronaut Teacher Christa McAuliffe*

- **Mad Dog!** - *Detroit Tiger Dick McAuliffe*

- **Charmed** - *From Motown to Combat & Back*

- **Almost** - *The Road to the Grande*

- **Thunder Road** - *Goodyear, God & Gatorade*

- **Buddy, Brian and Me** - *A Spooky Rock Story*

- **Frozen** - *A WWII and Mind over Matter Tale*

- **Soft Shell** - *Teddy the Talking Turtle*

- **Max and Me** - *Paws Across The Water*

- **Off the Rock** - *Escaping Alcatraz*

- **Deepwater Oil** - *Drillin on the Moon*

Books - eBooks - Audio Books
On sale at Amazon, Kindle, Apple iBooks, Barnes & Noble and your local independent book store!

Also Available at:
WWW.AUTHORTOMMCAULIFFE.COM

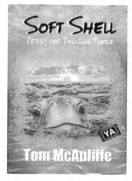

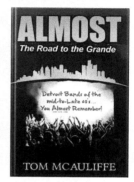

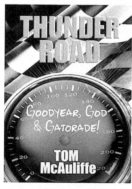

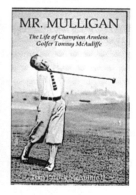

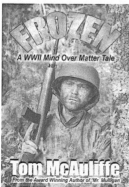

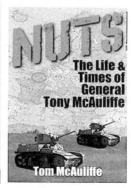

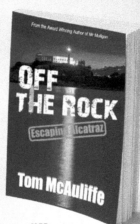

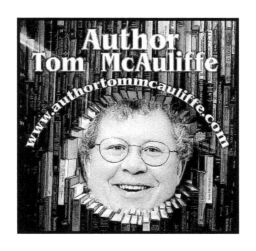

Please send questions to:
Bookinfo@nextstopparadise.com

Please Leave a Review!

Member:

Alliance of Independent Authors

Emerald Coast Writers

Military Photojournalists Association

Florida Writers Association